STEEL ON STEEL

A couple of feet away, the fallen gunman was gasping for breath. As Fargo started to get up, the man saw him and clawed at the handle of a knife sheathed at his hip.

Fargo swung a punch, driving his fist against the man's jaw. The blow sent the man rolling across the dirt, but he managed to pluck the knife from its sheath and slashed at Fargo with it. Fargo had to jerk back to avoid the deadly blade.

As he came to his feet, he reached down and pulled the Arkansas toothpick from the sheath strapped to his right calf. He straightened as the other man scrambled up and rushed at him, thrusting wildly with his knife. Fargo parried with the toothpick. The blades rang together, and sparks shot from cold steel as they clashed. . . .

THE TRAILSMAN

#297

SOUTH TEXAS SLAUGHTER

by

Jon Sharpe

A SIGNET BOOK

SIGNET
Published by New American Library, a division of
Penguin Group (USA) Inc., 375 Hudson Street,
New York, New York 10014, USA
Penguin Group (Canada), 90 Eglinton Avenue East, Suite 700, Toronto,
Ontario M4P 2Y3, Canada (a division of Pearson Penguin Canada Inc.)
Penguin Books Ltd., 80 Strand, London WC2R 0RL, England
Penguin Ireland, 25 St. Stephen's Green, Dublin 2,
Ireland (a division of Penguin Books Ltd.)
Penguin Group (Australia), 250 Camberwell Road, Camberwell, Victoria 3124,
Australia (a division of Pearson Australia Group Pty. Ltd.)
Penguin Books India Pvt. Ltd., 11 Community Centre, Panchsheel Park,
New Delhi - 110 017, India
Penguin Group (NZ), cnr Airborne and Rosedale Roads, Albany,
Auckland 1310, New Zealand (a division of Pearson New Zealand Ltd.)
Penguin Books (South Africa) (Pty.) Ltd., 24 Sturdee Avenue,
Rosebank, Johannesburg 2196, South Africa

Penguin Books Ltd., Registered Offices:
80 Strand, London WC2R 0RL, England

First published by Signet, an imprint of New American Library,
a division of Penguin Group (USA) Inc.

First Printing, July 2006
10 9 8 7 6 5 4 3 2 1

The first chapter of this book previously appeared in *Six-Gun Persuasion*, the
two hundred ninety-sixth volume in this series.

Copyright © Penguin Group (USA) Inc., 2006
All rights reserved

 REGISTERED TRADEMARK—MARCA REGISTRADA

Printed in the United States of America

The Trailsman

Beginnings . . . they bend the tree and they mark the man. Skye Fargo was born when he was eighteen. Terror was his midwife, vengeance his first cry. Killing spawned Skye Fargo, ruthless, cold-blooded murder. Out of the acrid smoke of gunpowder still hanging in the air, he rose, cried out a promise never forgotten.

The Trailsman they began to call him all across the West: searcher, scout, hunter, the man who could see where others only looked, his skills for hire but not his soul, the man who lived each day to the fullest, yet trailed each tomorrow. Skye Fargo, the Trailsman, the seeker who could take the wildness of a land and the wanting of a woman and make them his own.

*South Texas, 1860—where danger and death lurk
in the thorny thickets of the brush country.*

1

Leaning forward in the saddle as bullets whistled around his head, the big man in buckskins urged the stallion forward. The magnificent black-and-white Ovaro responded gallantly, as he always did, stretching his legs as he galloped along the winding trail through the chaparral.

Skye Fargo cast a glance over his shoulder, his lake blue eyes narrowing as he saw his pursuers race around a bend in the trail and thunder after him. The guns in their hands spouted flame. Lucky for Fargo, it was difficult to aim very accurately from the saddle of a galloping horse.

Running away stuck in his craw. It was his way to stand up to trouble whenever, wherever, and however it confronted him. He had always been that way, and although still a relatively young man, he was too old to change now.

One man against six heavily armed hombres who wanted to kill him wasn't a fight, though—it was suicide. Fargo was too smart to buck those odds, so when the half-dozen gunnies had spurred out of the brush behind him while he was riding along peacefully and opened fire on him, he did the only sensible thing.

He got the hell out of there.

Unfortunately, the men had come after him, still blazing away. Fargo had no idea who they were or why they wanted him dead, but it didn't seem to be the right time and place for asking questions.

The stallion whirled around another bend, momentarily cutting Fargo off from the sight of the rampaging gunmen. He glanced to both right and left in search of some place where he could turn and maybe throw them off his trail, but there was no place to go. The mesquite thickets were virtually impenetrable. Plunging into them would mean that both Fargo and the Ovaro would be clawed to ribbons by the thorny plants.

So all he could do was keep running, no matter how much it went against the grain. Either that, or stop and fight it out against overwhelming odds.

Suddenly, as he rounded another bend, an obstacle appeared in front of him. An old man was driving a wagon along the trail, whipping up a team of mules in an attempt to make them go faster. He threw a frantic look over his shoulder as Fargo approached.

Fargo realized that the old-timer must have heard the shooting behind him and wanted to get away, but he had the same problem—there was nowhere to go in this brasada except along the trail. The band of chaparral would end eventually, but too late to do any good for anyone caught in it by the gang of killers.

If those gunmen were willing to cut him down for no apparent reason, Fargo figured they wouldn't spare the old man, either. As he galloped toward the wagon, a plan formed in his head . . . not much of one, but maybe the only chance they would have.

The mules were no match for the Ovaro's speed. Fargo caught up quickly, rode past the wagon, and leaned over to grab the harness on one of the leaders. He reined in and hauled back on the harness with all his considerable strength, turning the mules toward the side of the trail and then bringing them to a halt.

"Dadgum it!" the old-timer on the wagon seat screeched at him. "What the hell do you think you're doin'?"

"Saving our lives, I hope," Fargo told him as he dropped from the stallion's back and pulled his Henry rifle from its saddle sheath. He slapped the Ovaro lightly on the rump and sent the black-and-white horse running around the wagon, which had come to a stop sitting at a slant across the trail.

The back of the wagon held bales of cotton wrapped in jute. That would give Fargo and the old-timer a little shelter from the bullets of the gunmen.

The would-be killers came around the bend and charged toward the wagon. There was no time to waste. Fargo vaulted to the seat, grabbed the old man's stringy arm, and leaped to the ground on the far side of the wagon, pulling the codger along with him. The old-timer yelped in alarm.

"Better pull that hogleg and give me a hand," Fargo said as bullets thudded into the cotton bales and the wooden frame of the wagon. He laid the barrel of the Henry over one of the bales and returned fire, cranking off five shots as fast as he could work the repeater's lever.

Beside him, the old man drew a long-barreled cap-and-ball revolver from a holster at his waist and joined Fargo in firing at their attackers. The heavy roar of the handgun was a sharp contrast to the whipcrack of the rifle.

Like all would-be killers, the gunmen didn't care for it when their intended victims fought back. They reined in as Fargo's slugs and the massive lead balls from the old-timer's pistol began to claw at them. One man swayed in the saddle, dropped his gun, and clapped a hand to his shoulder, which was suddenly bloody where a bullet from the Henry had torn through it.

The wounded gunman managed to stay mounted as the men wheeled their horses and fled. They didn't go far, though, just back around the bend in the trail where they were out of sight from the wagon. As Fargo and the old man held their fire, Fargo heard the hoofbeats stop short, and he had a pretty good idea what the men were up to.

Sure enough, a moment later more shots came from the thorny brush right at the bend. The men had dismounted, crawled back up to where they could draw a bead on the wagon, and opened fire again.

"What'll we do now?" the old-timer asked. "We could send a few howlin' blue whistlers into that brush, but we can't see what we'd be shootin' at!"

"And if you get back on that wagon seat, they'll pick you off," Fargo said. He knew that with the wagon blocking the trail, he could get on the Ovaro and probably make it away safely, shielded by the vehicle, but that would mean abandoning the old man.

Fargo wasn't about to do that. He rose up from behind the cotton bales long enough to throw two shots into the thickets, then ducked down again.

"Looks like we've got a standoff," he said. "Maybe they'll get tired of trying to kill us after a while."

The old man snorted. " 'Tain't likely. Did you see that big jigger in front? That was Johnny Lobo."

4

Fargo frowned over at the old man as bullets continued to smack into the wagon.

"Yeah, I know it's a damned silly name, but that's what he calls hisself. Since he heads up a bunch o' the most bloodthirsty cutthroats you'll find in these parts, not too many folks make fun of him for it."

Fargo recalled getting a pretty good look at the man the old-timer was talking about. The outlaw leader sat tall and powerful in the saddle, with a barrel chest and a bristling black beard. He'd had a colorful serape draped around his broad shoulders, and the wide-brimmed hat on his head was more piratical than the usual straw or felt sombrero.

"So you don't think this Johnny Lobo will give up and ride away, eh?"

"Especially not after you ventilated one o' his men. He'll want your blood now, for damn sure."

"Why did they open fire on me in the first place? I'm a stranger in these parts."

"Easiest kind to kill and rob." The old man jerked his head toward the Ovaro. "I expect once Johnny caught sight o' that horse o' yours, he wanted it bad. He's got an eye for horseflesh, Johnny does, and that stallion is one fine specimen."

Fargo couldn't argue with that. He and the Ovaro had been together for a lot of years and a lot of miles. The bond between them was more like that between brothers than that of man and horse.

"Well, I don't like it," the old man went on with a sigh, "but I reckon there's only one thing we can do." He took a flask from his pocket, along with flint and steel. "Get ready to jump on that long-legged hoss o' yours and ride, son."

"What are you going to do?" Fargo asked.

"Hide an' watch."

The smell of raw whiskey filled the air as the old

man uncorked the flask and doused a corner of one of the cotton bales. He struck a spark, and the whiskey-soaked cotton caught fire with a *whoosh*!

Fargo immediately saw what the old man's plan was. The tightly packed cotton wouldn't burn very fast, but thick, grayish-white smoke began to rise from the smoldering bale and the jute covering wrapped around it. The breeze from the south carried it toward the hidden gunmen.

"That's not much of a smoke screen," Fargo warned.

"Best I can do. Let's get outta here!"

Johnny Lobo and his outlaws were still firing, but as the smoke continued to thicken, they couldn't see as well what they were shooting at. Fargo had to fire blindly, too, but he laid down some cover with the Henry as the old man scrambled onto the wagon seat and grabbed the reins. As the old-timer whipped his team into motion, Fargo backed toward the Ovaro.

He reached the stallion and swung up into the saddle with the rifle still clutched in his right hand. The old man had the wagon moving now, and the wind whipped at the burning cotton bale and made the flames even stronger. Fargo held the Ovaro in and rode alongside the wagon. Smoke clogged the trail behind them.

"Will Lobo come after us?" Fargo called over the rattle of hoofbeats.

"Prob'ly! But we'll be outta this damn chaparral in another half mile!"

Fargo twisted in the saddle and fired the Henry a couple of times, not expecting to hit anything, just wanting to further discourage any more pursuit. The old-timer yelled curses at his mule team and urged more speed out of the animals.

The thickets began to thin out on both sides of the

trail. After a few more minutes, Fargo and the old man emerged from the chaparral into a sandy, mostly flat countryside covered with hardy grass and dotted with clumps of scrub brush. Off to the west of this trail that ran from San Antonio to Corpus Christi on the Gulf of Mexico, a line of trees marked the course of the Nueces River.

The old-timer leaned back on the seat and hauled on the reins, yelling, "Whoa, you damn jugheads, whoa!" The mules gradually came to a stop.

Smoke still billowed from the burning cotton bale, but the fire hadn't spread to the other bales. Fargo stepped from the Ovaro's back into the wagon bed and put his shoulder to the burning bale along with the old man. Together, they shoved it out so that it fell in the trail, where the flames couldn't spread to the rest of the old-timer's cargo.

"Hate to lose part o' my shipment," the old man said, "but I reckon that's better'n gettin' shot to pieces by Johnny Lobo's gang."

Fargo kept a close eye on the spot where the trail emerged from the chaparral. He halfway expected to see the outlaws come galloping out of there, still intent on murder. So far, though, that hadn't happened.

"Let's keep moving," he suggested. "We need to put some distance between ourselves and that bunch."

"Amen," the old-timer said as he resumed his seat and took up the reins. "I'm a mite surprised Lobo ain't come after us yet."

So was Fargo, but he wasn't going to complain about good fortune. He mounted up again and, side by side, he and the old man struck a brisk pace down the trail, which was widening into a full-fledged road now that it was out of the brush.

"Name's Howard Jones," the old man said, "but they call me Rooster." He plucked the shapeless, bat-

7

tered old felt hat off his head, and Fargo saw where he had gotten the nickname. White hair stuck up like the comb on a rooster's head.

"Pleased to meet you, Rooster," Fargo said, "although I might wish it had been under better circumstances. I'm Skye Fargo."

"You bound for Corpus Christi? That's about the only good-sized town in the direction we're goin'."

Fargo nodded. "That's right."

"Me, too. Got to deliver this load o' cotton there, to be shipped out to England. I take cotton reg'lar to Corpus for the planters up around San Antone and Seguin."

Fargo didn't explain his reasons for going to Corpus Christi, and in truth, he didn't have any pressing business there. He was drifting, and he hadn't been to South Texas in a while. That was reason enough in itself for the trip. If the notion struck him, he might ride on down to Mexico, even though there were some places there where gringos weren't very welcome. A lot of bitterness remained from the war with the United States a dozen years earlier, and the Texas Revolution before that.

Indulging his curiosity, Fargo said, "Tell me about this Johnny Lobo."

"He's the worst outlaw these parts have seen for a long time. Tell you the truth, I was a mite worried about comin' through here with this cotton. Figure Lobo and his bunch would've left me alone, though, if they hadn't been chasin' you."

"Sorry," Fargo said.

"Hell, 'tain't your fault. Just my bad luck I happened to be on the trail when you fellas come skalley-hootin' along there, burnin' powder. It was just a good thing Lobo didn't have his whole bunch with him."

"There are more of them?"

"Hell, yes," Rooster said. "Lobo's got at least a couple o' dozen tough hombres ridin' with him. Some of 'em come up from below the border, but the rest are homegrown owlhoots. They've raided quite a few ranches, held up the stagecoach between Victoria and Corpus a heap o' times, and robbed and killed more folks than I like to think about."

"Sounds like the law ought to do something about him."

Rooster snorted. "What law? There's a sheriff down at Corpus, but up here in the brasada . . . nada."

Fargo chuckled. "What about the Rangers?"

"They ain't much count, 'cept for Rip Ford and his company, and they're down along the Rio Grande right now, a long ways from here. It's like things always are on the frontier . . . folks got to take care o' themselves and handle their own problems."

Fargo nodded slowly. In his wanderings, he had been in plenty of places where there was no real law. Outlaws like Johnny Lobo and his bunch tended to congregate in those areas, thinking that they would find the settlers to be easy pickings. In most cases they were right.

But the pioneers who ventured out into the mostly uncivilized places were a hardy breed, too, and they fought back when they could. Fargo was confident that eventually they would turn the tide of lawlessness and build something lasting and worthwhile, would turn the wild frontier into a place where folks could raise their families in peace.

Those days, if they ever came, were still a long way off, though, and it sounded to Fargo as if the people who lived in this brushy country along the Nueces needed a hand. He wasn't in any hurry to get anywhere. Maybe he would stick around for a while and see if there was anything he could do to help.

It was getting late in the afternoon. They wouldn't reach Corpus Christi today, and might not the next day. Fargo said to Rooster, "I reckon you'll be looking for a place to camp."

"Nope, already got one," the old-timer replied. "I know right where I'm goin'. I always spend a night with the Barrientos when I come through here."

"The Barrientos? Who's that?"

"Family o' mustangers. They got a camp up here, not far down the road." Rooster licked his lips. "Mighty fine food, and they're friendly folks. I don't reckon they'd mind havin' a little extra comp'ny for the night."

Fargo was about to say that sounded fine to him when a gunshot shattered the late afternoon quiet. At the same time, he heard the distinctive thud of lead against flesh, and Rooster grunted in pain.

Twisting in the saddle, Fargo saw Rooster doubled over on the wagon seat, clutching his side. At the same time, a rifle blasted again, and Fargo spotted the puff of smoke from a nearby clump of cottonwood trees as he heard the wind-rip of the bullet past his ear.

There was no time to see how badly Rooster was hurt. The bushwhacker had to be dealt with first. Fargo jerked the Henry from its sheath and returned fire as another slug screamed past him. He snapped off a couple of shots and then kicked the stallion into a run toward the trees.

The sight of Fargo charging the cottonwoods like that must have unnerved the bushwhacker because the man bolted from his concealment and galloped toward the Nueces on the back of a gray horse. Fargo recalled seeing the horse a short time earlier. One of the men who had tried to kill him had been riding it.

Fargo closed in quickly on the fleeing gunman. He wanted to take the man alive, so that he could ask him some questions—like why Johnny Lobo was so determined to kill a stranger. Of course, Rooster might be right. It might be a simple case of attempted robbery, horse theft, and murder. But Fargo wanted to make sure nothing else was going on.

The bushwhacker twisted in his saddle and fired back at Fargo with a handgun. The shots went wild, but Fargo leaned forward in the saddle to make himself a smaller target anyway. The Ovaro slowly drew closer to the gray. Fargo was close enough now to see the fearful expression in his quarry's eyes when the man glanced back again. With fumbling fingers, the bushwhacker was trying to reload the revolver he had emptied.

The stallion drew alongside the other horse. Fargo launched himself from the saddle in a diving tackle. He hit the gunman solidly and drove him off the back of the gray. Both men tumbled to the ground, landing hard.

Fargo rolled over. The impact had knocked his wide-brimmed brown hat to the ground. He tossed his head a little to get his thick black hair out of his eyes. A couple of feet away, the fallen gunman was gasping for breath. As Fargo started to get up, the man saw him and clawed at the handle of a knife sheathed at his hip.

Fargo swung a punch, driving his fist against the man's jaw. The blow sent the man rolling across the dirt, but he managed to pluck the knife from its sheath and slashed at Fargo with it. Fargo had to jerk back to avoid the deadly blade.

As he came to his feet, he reached down and pulled his Arkansas toothpick from the sheath strapped to his right calf. He straightened as the other man scrambled up and rushed at him, thrusting wildly with his knife. Fargo parried with the toothpick. The blades rang together, and sparks shot from cold steel as they clashed.

Fargo had been in many knife fights over the years, and he saw quickly that his opponent was too undisciplined, too panic-stricken, to win. Fargo could have killed him a couple of times during the opening minutes of the fight. For that matter, he could have pulled the Colt on his hip and shot the man.

But he still didn't want that. He fought defensively, drawing his opponent in, hoping to disarm the man without wounding him seriously.

The bushwhacker was a Mexican, a wiry, bearded hardcase with ruthless cruelty in his eyes. He must have split off from the rest of Lobo's gang and circled around to get in front of Fargo and Rooster. Maybe Lobo had ordered him to ambush them, or maybe he had done it on his own, hoping to impress the leader of the gang by killing the two men who had gotten away from them in the chaparral. If Fargo was able to end this fight the way he wanted, he ought to be able to find out the answers to those questions.

Another worry began to nag at Fargo's brain. He didn't know how badly Rooster was hurt. The old-timer might be bleeding to death right now, and need immediate medical attention. There was also the possibility that the rest of the gang might catch up to the wagon.

All in all, Fargo knew that he had to go ahead and end this fight as quickly as he could, while still trying to capture the bushwhacker without killing him.

With a snarl on his lips, the bushwhacker charged again. Fargo caught the man's knife on the long, heavy blade of the Arkansas toothpick, slid the blade along his enemy's steel until the hilts locked, and then, with a twist of his powerful wrist, tore the knife loose from the man's hand. The man cursed in Spanish and lunged at Fargo, trying to get a hand on his throat, but Fargo sidestepped, stuck a booted foot between the man's calves, and tripped him. The man flopped face-first on the ground.

When a thin scream came from the man's lips and he began to writhe on the ground, Fargo knew something unforeseen had happened. He leaned down, grabbed the bushwhacker's shoulder, and rolled him onto his back. The handle of the man's knife jutted up from his chest.

Fargo's mouth tightened into a grim line. It was clear what had happened—when the bushwhacker dropped his knife, it had landed with the blade pointing up, and the man had fallen on it when Fargo tripped him. The impact had driven the blade deep into the man's chest.

As Fargo watched, blood trickled from the bushwhacker's mouth. He arched his back and tried to say something, but his voice was choked and Fargo didn't understand anything except *"Dios mio!"* Then the man slumped and the life went out of his eyes.

Fargo bit back a curse. He wished things hadn't turned out this way, but he wasn't going to stand around brooding about it. The bushwhacker had tried to kill him, after all, and right now Fargo was more worried about Rooster Jones.

He slipped the toothpick back in its sheath and whistled for the Ovaro. The big stallion trotted up as Fargo was retrieving his hat. Leaving the dead bushwhacker and the man's horse where they were, Fargo mounted quickly and hurried back to the road.

Fargo didn't see any sign of the rest of the gang as he approached Rooster's wagon. The old-timer still sat hunched over on the seat. He lifted his head as Fargo rode up, though, so he was still alive and conscious.

"How bad is it?" Fargo asked as he swung down from the saddle.

"Hurts like blazes, but I don't reckon it'll kill me," Rooster replied through gritted teeth. "The slug tore a chunk o' meat outta my side, but it missed my vitals."

Fargo said, "Let me take a look. I've had a little experience patching up bullet holes."

Rooster grunted. "Yeah, you seem like the sorta fella who would have. I'll be all right if you just get me to the Barrientos' camp. Old Eduardo was a sawbones in Mexico 'fore he took up mustangin'."

That seemed like an odd switch, going from being a doctor to catching wild mustangs, but Fargo didn't say anything about it. He said, "Move over a little. I'll handle the team."

While Rooster slid over on the seat and grunted in pain at the movement, Fargo tied the Ovaro to the rear of the wagon. The stallion could follow along behind while Fargo drove the vehicle.

Fargo climbed to the seat and took up the reins. He flapped them and got the mules moving. As the wagon lurched into motion, Rooster asked, "Who was that son of a bitch, and what happened to him? I heard more shootin'."

"He was one of Lobo's gang. I recognized his horse, and I think I remember seeing him while they were chasing me. I tried to take him alive so I could ask him some questions, but we wound up fighting with knives, and he fell on his."

"Askin' questions of one o' those rapscallions would be a waste o' time and breath. He never would've admitted to nothin'. Prob'ly too scared o' Lobo to talk."

"Runs the gang with an iron fist, does he?"

Rooster nodded. "From what I've heard. I wouldn't know for sure, o' course." The old man was quiet for a moment, then went on, "He must've rode like hell to get around us and set up that ambush."

"Maybe he had the fastest horse and Lobo sent him to slow us down," Fargo said.

Rooster lifted a hand and pointed. Fargo couldn't help but see the blood on the old man's hand where he'd had it pressed to the wound in his side. "The camp's up yonder, off to the left side o' the road in them trees."

The sun was almost down now, and the dusk was thickening enough so that Fargo could see the flickering of a campfire in the trees Rooster had indicated. He followed the road a short distance farther, then swung the wagon off of it and headed for the grove.

He hadn't quite gotten there when a voice suddenly called warningly, "Hold it right there, señor, or I'll blow your head off!"

2

The voice belonged to a woman, and a fairly young one, from the sound of it. Fargo couldn't see her and didn't know if she was pointing a gun at him or not, but he hauled back on the reins anyway, figuring there wasn't any point in taking a chance. The wagon came to a stop.

Beside him on the seat, Rooster lifted his head and called, "Take it easy on that trigger finger, Elena. It's me, Rooster Jones, and I'm hurt."

In a low voice, Fargo asked, "You reckon she's really got a gun?"

The old-timer snorted. "Damn right she's got a gun. Knows how to use it, too. Eduardo made sure all his gals could shoot."

The next moment, the young woman in question hurried out of the trees and ran toward the wagon. Sure enough, she had a rifle in one hand. As she came up, she said, "Oh, Rooster! How bad are you hurt?"

He grinned as she reached up and laid a concerned

hand on his leg. "Got a pretty deep bullet crease in my side, but I'm feelin' a mite better now."

Fargo could see why a little attention from this young woman would make most men feel better, even ones who had been shot. Elena Barrientos was truly lovely, with long, thick, dark brown hair, smooth skin that seemed to glow golden in the fading light, and a supple figure that was displayed very fetchingly in tight denim trousers and a man's butternut shirt. A brown felt sombrero hung behind her head by its chinstrap.

In addition to the rifle she carried, she wore a gun belt strapped around her hips like a man. No man ever had hips that curved quite so sensuously, though. Fargo wondered if she could use the six-shooter that jutted up from the holster. After what Rooster had said, he was willing to bet that she could.

"Let me help you down and get you into camp," Elena went on. "Papa isn't here right now, but he should be back soon. He'll take care of you."

"Much obliged."

Fargo started to swing down on the other side of the seat, but he froze as Elena suddenly palmed out the revolver and pointed it at him. She was pretty fast on the draw. "I didn't say *you* could get down, señor."

Fargo didn't like having a gun pointed at him, even when it was in the hand of a pretty girl. He was about to say as much, but Rooster interceded first.

"Put that smokepole away, Elena," the old man said. "This here is Skye Fargo. He's a friend of mine, I reckon. Saved my bacon from Johnny Lobo."

Elena's dark eyes widened. "Lobo!" she repeated. "That hombre is around here?"

"Yep. Seen him with my own eyes. Prob'ly would've killed me and stole all this cotton if it hadn't been for Fargo." Rooster chuckled. "O' course, Lobo and his bunch might not have bothered me if they hadn't been tryin' to kill Fargo first."

Elena holstered her gun with a move as smooth as the one that had drawn it. "My apologies, señor," she said as she looked at Fargo. Her eyes played over his buckskin-clad form in evident approval, to judge from the smoldering look he saw there. "Any enemy of Johnny Lobo's is an amigo to the Barrientos family."

Fargo smiled slightly. "That's just it," he said. "I didn't know I was one of Johnny Lobo's enemies until he and his men started shooting at me. I'd never heard of him until today."

"You are fortunate, then. Give me a hand with Rooster."

Fargo hopped down from the seat, went around the back of the wagon, and helped Elena assist Rooster to the ground. Then, while Elena went ahead, Fargo helped the old-timer into the woods.

The Barrientos camp was surprisingly large, with four tents scattered around a clearing in the trees that would provide shade during the day. A couple of wagons were parked nearby, and the horses that made up their teams grazed inside a rope corral. A regular table and chairs, as would be found in a house, were set up between the fire and one of the wagons.

"Looks like home away from home," Fargo commented.

"We are out for weeks, sometimes months, searching for wild horses," Elena said. "My father believes man should not do completely without creature comforts, no matter what the circumstances."

"Your father is a wise man."

"Very wise," Elena agreed. "Rooster, sit down there at the table."

As Fargo helped Rooster settle onto a chair, the entrance flap on one of the tents was thrown back, and another woman stepped out into the dusk. The light from the fire washed over her, and Fargo couldn't help but be surprised at how beautiful she was. Considerably older than Elena, she was still very attractive, with hair the color of honey. Her eyes were dark, though, and Fargo recognized a Castilian accent as she said, "Elena, what is wrong with Señor Rooster?"

"He has been shot, Mama," Elena replied, "by one of Johnny Lobo's men."

The woman crossed herself and said something under her breath that Fargo took to be a prayer. Obviously, the mention of Johnny Lobo had spooked her.

"Howdy, Señora Barrientos," Rooster said. "Sorry to intrude on you like this."

"It is no intrusion," the woman said as she came to the table and rested a hand lightly on Rooster's shoulder. "Eduardo will be here soon. Is there anything we can do for you until then?"

"Well . . . my flask is empty, so if you've got a jug o' sangria wine around . . ."

"Of course." Señora Barrientos turned to her daughter. "Elena, fetch wine for our guests."

Elena nodded and went toward one of the wagons. Rooster went on, "Señora, this here is Skye Fargo. He lent me a hand and brung me here."

The woman smiled warmly at Fargo. At first he had thought that she wasn't old enough to have a daughter as old as Elena, but now he saw that she had simply aged very well, as women of pure Spanish blood often do. She must have come to Mexico as a young woman, he thought, since she retained that touch of Castile in her voice, even when speaking English.

"Señor Fargo," she said as she extended a hand to him. "Welcome to our camp."

He wasn't sure if he was supposed to shake her hand or kiss the back of it. He settled for shaking it, since he wasn't a European, and said, "It's my honor to be here, señora. Thank you for your hospitality."

"I am Juliana Barrientos. You have already met my daughter Elena, I take it."

"Yes, ma'am, I've had the pleasure."

"What is this about Johnny Lobo?" As she asked the question, her hand moved a little, as if she wanted to make the sign of the cross again but restrained herself.

"He and some of his men jumped me while I was riding through the chaparral," Fargo explained. "While I was trying to get away from them, I caught up with Rooster's wagon and the gang opened fire on him, too. We had to work together to get away from the outlaws. Then, after we'd gotten out of the chaparral and thought we had lost Lobo's bunch, one of them bushwhacked us and wounded Rooster."

"How terrible," Juliana Barrientos murmured. "How badly is Señor Jones injured?"

Rooster put in, "Not too bad. I won't be very spry for a few days, but I reckon I'll be all right."

"Thank the Blessed Virgin for that."

Elena returned with a jug of wine and a couple of clay cups that she filled for Fargo and Rooster. Juliana went on. "You will spend the night with us, of course. Perhaps longer, if you need the rest, Señor Jones."

"I'm obliged for that hospitable offer, señora, but I got to get that load o' cotton to Corpus Christi as soon as I can."

Fargo was about to offer to take the cotton on to the seaport town, when the sudden drumming of hoofbeats not far away made everyone look up. Fargo immediately thought about the outlaw gang, but after a second he realized he was hearing only one horse.

The approaching rider might still be a threat. Fargo set his cup of wine on the table and turned toward the sound, his right hand hovering over the butt of the Colt. Likewise, Elena lifted her rifle and stood ready for trouble.

A clear, feminine voice rang through the trees. "Mama! Elena! Thieves are after the herd!"

"Dios mio!" Juliana exclaimed as her hand went to her throat. A second later the rider galloped into the firelight and pulled her horse to a skidding halt.

After everything that had happened already, Fargo wasn't really surprised to see that the rider was a beautiful young woman. He remembered, too, that Rooster had made it sound like Eduardo Barrientos had more than one daughter. Fargo figured this new-comer was another Barrientos daughter, and he didn't know if that was all of them or not.

The girl was younger than Elena, probably no more than eighteen, but she was just as lovely, with raven hair and olive skin and a lithe figure. The family re-semblance in their faces was obvious. She wore denim trousers and a man's shirt like her sister, but no gun belt. The stock of a rifle jutted up from a saddle sheath on her horse.

She barely spared a glance for Fargo and Rooster as she hurried over to her mother. "Papa and Tony are trying to hold them off and keep them from steal-ing the herd," she babbled, "but we must help!"

Juliana gripped her younger daughter's arms. "Ra-mona, control yourself! Who is after the herd?"

The answer didn't come as a surprise to Fargo, ei-ther. "Johnny Lobo!" Ramona Barrientos gasped.

"Impossible! He has never bothered us before!"

"I saw it with my own eyes, Mama," Ramona in-sisted. "I was riding back to the holding corral when I heard the shots. I galloped to where I could see Papa and Tony, but they waved me away and Papa shouted for me to get help. Please! There is no time—"

"Show me where the herd is," Fargo broke in. "I'll help you."

Ramona turned frightened eyes toward him. "Who are you, señor?"

"A friend," Elena said quickly as she led up a saddled horse from the rope corral. "Come, Señor Fargo. Mama will stay here with Señor Rooster."

Her voice held a rather imperious tone of command, but Fargo didn't argue with her. It was more important to get to the herd of mustangs that the Barrientos family had gathered, and stop Johnny Lobo from grabbing it. He took hold of the Ovaro's reins and swung up into the saddle as Elena was getting mounted on her horse.

"Be careful!" Juliana called after them as Fargo and the two sisters galloped out of the camp. They struck off toward the west, heading cross-country rather than following the road.

Fargo had already noticed that the mustang herd wasn't being held near the camp. The family had a holding area elsewhere, probably in a place that was more geographically suited for such a purpose. It wouldn't be very far off, though.

The moon was rising when they reached the Nueces River a few minutes later. Ramona had led them unerringly to a spot where the stream could be forded. As the horses splashed across the ford, Fargo began to hear a popping sound that could only be gunshots. Eduardo Barrientos and someone called Tony, perhaps his son, were still defending the herd from the outlaws who wanted to grab it.

The shots grew louder as Fargo, Elena, and Ramona approached. Fargo saw a dark line ahead that he recognized as a low bluff. As they came closer and the silvery wash of light from the rising moon grew

22

stronger, he could make out a brush fence that had been erected to form a large enclosure, with the bluff forming the rear wall of the roughly square corral.

The flame of a gunshot bloomed in the darkness, stabbing out in a couple of places from behind the thorny barricade. More muzzle flashes spouted from outside the fence as the outlaws poured lead at the defenders. They had left their saddles and were hunkered down behind scrub bushes and sandy knolls. Fargo could tell there were at least a dozen attackers. They had the holding corral pretty well surrounded.

Even with Fargo and the two girls arriving as reinforcements, the odds against them would still be more than two to one. But he and his companions had the element of surprise on their side, plus they would have the outlaws between two fires.

"Spread out and charge them," he called, not worrying about stepping on Elena's toes by giving orders. "Pepper them with rifle fire as hard as you can!"

He took the center of the attack, with Ramona peeling off to the right and Elena to the left. The outlaws were concentrating on the corral, so they didn't hear the hoofbeats of the approaching horses until they were fairly close. Fargo pulled the Ovaro to a halt, brought the Henry to his shoulder, and opened fire.

As they were riding up he had marked the locations of the outlaws' muzzle flashes as best he could in his mind, so his shots were remarkably accurate as he cranked them off. He fired, shifted his aim as he levered another round into the Henry's chamber, and fired again. Some fifty yards distant on either side of him, Elena and Ramona were doing the same thing.

The would-be horse thieves didn't take long to respond to the attack. Unfortunately for several of them, they leaped up as they spun around to return Fargo's fire, making them better targets. He saw a couple of them driven off their feet by his slugs, and a couple more staggered, obviously hit.

"Come on!" Fargo heard a deep voice bellow to his right. "Let's get out of here, boyos!"

The accent wasn't Mexican. In fact, it sounded odd to Fargo's ears. But the unmistakable tone of command in it made him think that it belonged to Johnny Lobo. Fargo wheeled the stallion in that direction. His keen eyes spotted a massive figure pulling itself onto a horse.

Fargo snapped off a shot at Lobo and saw the big man jerk. Whether he was hit or not, though, Lobo managed to grab leather and settle himself in the saddle. The horse plunged away into the night as he raked its flanks with his spurs. Fargo threw another shot after the fleeing bandit chief, but was pretty sure he missed.

The other outlaws who weren't either dead or wounded too badly to move were taking off for the tall and uncut, too. Fargo, Elena, and Ramona hurried them along with a few last shots, then headed for the corral.

"Hold your fire, Papa!" Elena called.

Fargo and the two young women converged on a gate in the front wall of the holding corral. The gate swung open and a stocky man with a rifle in his hands stepped out to meet them. "Ramona! Elena!" he called. "Are you all right?"

"Fine, Papa," Elena said as she dismounted. Ramona echoed the response. Elena waved a hand at Fargo. "This is Señor Fargo, a friend of Señor Rooster. He came along to help us."

Eduardo Barrientos strode forward to extend a hand to Fargo, who had swung down from the back of the Ovaro. The man was middle-aged and a little below medium height, with a close-cropped beard. Unlike his daughters, whose range garb was more typically American, he dressed like a vaquero, in a charro jacket and tight trousers, with a wide-brimmed, steeple-crowned sombrero on his head.

"Señor Fargo," he said as he shook hands. "Gracias, señor, for your help! If you and my daughters had not arrived when you did, we would not have been able to drive those devils off!"

"I'm glad I was here to lend a hand," Fargo said. He felt an instinctive liking for Barrientos. "That was Johnny Lobo's bunch, wasn't it?"

"*Sí.* You know about Johnny Lobo?"

"I'm learning," Fargo said, a grim tone edging into his voice, "and I don't much like what I hear about him."

"He is an hombre *muy malo.* A very bad man. He and his men hit us right after dark. Thank the Blessed Virgin that Lobo did not wait a short time longer to strike. If he had, my daughter Antonia would have been here alone, guarding the herd."

At Barrientos' words, yet another young woman walked out of the corral, a rifle tucked under her left arm. Like Elena and Ramona, she was dressed more like a Texas cowboy than a Mexican señorita. But when she took off the black hat she wore, long dark hair tumbled down her back. It was difficult to be certain in the moonlight, but Fargo would have been willing to bet that she was just as pretty as her sisters.

So "Tony" wasn't a Barrientos son after all. Fargo was beginning to wonder if Eduardo and Juliana even had any male offspring.

He looked past the gate and saw a dark mass inside the corral that represented a couple of dozen mustangs milling around, spooked by all the shooting. Catching the wild horses wasn't easy in the first place;

controlling them after they were caught was a hard chore, too. But once they were driven into a corral like this, they generally wouldn't try to bust out. They knew instinctively to stay away from the walls of thorny mesquite.

"Have you had trouble with Lobo and his gang before?" Fargo asked.

Barrientos shook his head. "Never. Perhaps that made us overconfident. Because Lobo has always left us alone, perhaps we thought that he always would."

That was yet another oddity, Fargo told himself. From what Rooster Jones had told him about Lobo, the bandit chief and his men had cut a wide bloody swath through the Nueces country. It didn't make sense that they would ignore the Barrientos family's mustanging operation. Those wild horses could be sold for a good price in San Antonio, or below the border if Lobo wanted to go that way.

Regardless of what had happened before, though, Eduardo Barrientos would no longer assume that he was safe from Johnny Lobo. Not after tonight.

"Elena said you are a friend of Señor Rooster," Barrientos went on. "Is he traveling with you?"

"Well, sort of," Fargo said. "We just met up earlier this afternoon, but it looks like we're going to be partners for a while." Fargo still felt a bit of indirect responsibility for that bullet crease in the old-timer's side, so he planned to look after Rooster until it healed up. "He's back in your camp now," Fargo went on, "and he could use some medical attention. I hear that you used to be a doctor."

Barrientos smiled sadly. "*Es verdad.* I was indeed a sawbones, as you Americans say. But political reverses, so common in my country, stripped my family of its wealth and position. We lost our home in Mexico City and were forced to move elsewhere and find an-

26

other way to live." He waved a hand at the corral. "Mustanging has become our life."

"I know how important these animals are to you and your family," Fargo said with a nod. "If you'll go back to your camp and tend to Rooster's wound, I'll stay here and stand guard all night."

"I will, of course, see to Señor Jones's wound," Barrientos said. "And I accept your kind offer, Señor Fargo. But you cannot stay here alone. One man would be no match for Lobo and his hombres if they come back."

Without hesitation, Antonia said, "I will stay with Señor Fargo."

"I should stand guard," Elena said. "I'm more rested than Tony."

"What about me?" Ramona put in. "I can shoot."

Sternly, Barrientos said, "You are too young. It would not be proper."

Ramona pointed at Elena. "She's only two years older than me!"

"And I have not said that she can stay," Barrientos replied. "Elena, you will come back to camp with Ramona and me. Antonia will stay and help Señor Fargo stand guard." He sighed a little. "That is not proper, either, of course, but a man blessed with only daughters soon learns that propriety is not always possible."

"Besides, I'm not a virgin whose virtue must be protected," Antonia said with a smug smile directed at her sisters.

"Antonia!" Barrientos said sharply. "I realize decorum is difficult in this . . . this wild brush country . . . but you must not be so brazen!"

"Sorry, Papa," she said with her eyes cast toward the ground. "I just thought that since I have been married, it would be less scandalous for me to remain with Señor Fargo."

"You're right, of course," Barrientos admitted, "and while we argue, Señor Rooster's condition may be worsening. Mount up, girls! We ride!"

Barrientos got a saddle horse that was tied near the corral while Elena and Ramona climbed back on their mounts. The three of them rode off quickly, heading east toward the family's camp on the other side of the Nueces.

Fargo tied the Ovaro's reins to a small cottonwood. Antonia came over to him and said, "We have not been properly introduced, Señor Fargo. I am Antonia Barrientos y Escobar."

"My pleasure, señora," Fargo murmured. "I believe you said that you're married?"

"I *was* married. My husband is dead."

"Oh. I'm sorry to hear that." He wondered what had happened, but it wouldn't be polite to ask.

Antonia supplied the answer anyway. "My husband Juan Pablo was put before a firing squad when the winds of political fortune changed in Mexico City, as my father mentioned. What he did not say was that he would have been next if we had not fled."

"That's too bad," Fargo said, and meant it. "At least you managed to make it to Texas."

"Yes. The life here may be hard, but at least no one tries to shoot us." She paused, then added, "Not until tonight, anyway."

The whole question of why Lobo had suddenly targeted the Barrientos family still nagged at Fargo's mind, but he pushed it aside. Right now he needed to concentrate on being alert for trouble.

"I think I'll go over there and sit in the shade of that cottonwood," he said. "That way, if anybody tries to sneak up on the corral, they won't be as likely to see me."

"And I will go inside the corral," Antonia said.

Now that he was closer, Fargo could see that the brush fence had two layers with a narrow walkway between them. That way defenders could crouch in the lane, as Barrientos and Antonia had done, without exposing themselves to the danger of being attacked by the wild horses. Those mustangs might regard a human being on foot as too tempting a target to resist, no matter what was going on.

Fargo settled down on the sandy ground with his back against the trunk of the cottonwood. The night was dark and warm and quiet, and he'd had a long, eventful day. Under those circumstances, some men would have had trouble staying awake.

Not Fargo, though, who had been conditioned by an eventful *life*, not just one day, to remain alert when he needed to be. There were limits beyond which even his iron constitution could not be pushed, but he was nowhere near them.

After an hour or so, the crunch of sand underfoot told him that someone was coming from the direction of the corral. He supposed it was Antonia, but he wasn't going to take any chances. He came silently to his feet and stood there, muscles tensed, the Henry rifle ready in his hands, in case of danger.

"Señor Fargo?"

The quiet voice told him he'd been right—it was Antonia. He asked, "What is it?"

She gasped a little and then turned toward him. "I did not see you there at all," she said. "You blend into the night like a . . . a wild animal."

Fargo ignored that comment. "There's no trouble?"

"No. I just thought perhaps we could sit together for a while. This brasada is a lonely place, especially at night."

Fargo couldn't argue with that statement. He relaxed and said, "Sure, sit down."

He hunkered on his heels and rested his back against the tree trunk. Antonia sat beside him. Quietly, she said, "You must tell me about yourself, Señor Fargo."

"There's not much to tell."

"Anyone can look at you and know that is not true. You have heard things about me. Now tell me, have *you* ever been married?"

Fargo chuckled. "Nope."

"Because you never found the right woman? You cannot tell me that you have no interest in women, because I know that would be a lie, too. I saw the way you looked at me, and at my sisters."

"I meant no offense," Fargo said.

"Of course not. Why would there be any offense in a normal man looking at a beautiful woman? My sisters are very lovely."

"Now you're fishing for a compliment," Fargo said, but his light tone robbed the words of any sting they might have had. "You're just as lovely as they are, and you know it. More lovely, perhaps, because life and experience can't help but make a woman more attractive."

She laughed, and the sound was like music in the night. "You are saying that I am old? It is true, I am older than Elena and Ramona. I am twenty-four. If things had been different, I would be a fat, happy, married woman by now, with babies at my feet."

Her tone was light and playful, but Fargo sensed an edge of sadness in her words. Life had taken some difficult turns for her and her family. That was one more reason he was determined that they wouldn't lose their herd to a bunch of no-account owlhoots like Lobo and his gang.

He turned to her and echoed his thoughts by saying,

"Life takes many turns. But it's brought us together, at this time and this place."

"Yes," Antonia breathed. "And for that, I think, we should be thankful."

She leaned toward him, and instinct guided both of them. Their lips came together, softly at first but then with more heat and urgency. They had known each other for only a very short time, and hadn't even seen each other in daylight yet, but that didn't matter. There had been one of those rare, immediate sparks between them, an element of attraction between this particular man and this particular woman that couldn't be denied. Fargo slipped his free arm around her and drew her closer, feeling the warmth of her lush body as she pressed against him.

There wasn't much telling what might have happened then—if they hadn't both heard the sudden thud of hoofbeats approaching in the night.

3

Fargo came quickly to his feet and Antonia scrambled upright beside him. Both of them lifted their rifles, ready to blast whoever was riding quickly toward the corral.

But then a familiar voice called, "Hola! Do not fire!"

"My father," Antonia breathed. She stepped forward.

Fargo stopped her with a hand on her shoulder. "Wait a minute," he said quietly. "Best make sure he's by himself and nobody's got a gun in his back, trying to make him throw us off guard."

"That would never happen," Antonia said. "Papa would die before he would betray his family."

But she waited anyway until Eduardo Barrientos came into view, alone. He rode up to the corral and dismounted as Fargo and Antonia came forward to greet him.

"Any trouble while I was gone?" he asked.

"None, Papa," Antonia answered. "The night is quiet and peaceful now. I thought that you would stay at the camp until morning."

"I grew concerned about you and Señor Fargo being out here alone," Barrientos said easily, "in case Johnny Lobo and his men came back, you know. So once I had attended to Señor Rooster's wound, I decided I should return and help you stand guard."

"That was a good idea, Señor Barrientos," Fargo replied, with an ease that matched the older man's.

"Yes," Antonia said, a little less graciously. "A good idea."

Barrientos unsaddled his horse and tied it under the scrubby cottonwoods with Fargo's stallion and Antonia's horse. He said to his daughter, "Why don't you brew some coffee while I talk to Señor Fargo?"

Muttering under her breath, she went off to rekindle the fire and put coffee on to boil. Fargo and Barrientos stood beside the gate with their rifles tucked under their arms.

"How was Rooster?" Fargo asked.

Barrientos laughed. "Talking a mile a minute, as usual. He will be fine. I cleaned and bandaged his wound. The blood made it look worse than it really was. He will be sore for a few weeks, but the bullet did not penetrate deeply enough to do any permanent damage."

"That's what I thought, too, but it's good to have it confirmed by somebody who knows what he's talking about. How soon will he be able to travel again?"

"Ah, now that may present a problem," Barrientos said. "Señor Rooster insists that he must deliver his load of cotton to Corpus Christi immediately, but he really needs to rest for at least four or five days before undertaking such a trip. It would be better if he waited

a week or even longer. But unless we tie him up"—
Barrientos shrugged eloquently—"I fear that he will
leave in the morning and put his recovery in danger."

Fargo mulled that over for a few moments. He was
in a bad position here. He wanted to help Rooster by
taking the cotton on to Corpus Christi, but at the same
time he thought that the Barrientos family might need
him to stay and help them protect their herd from
Johnny Lobo.

Maybe the two chores could be combined. "How
soon will you be ready to drive those mustangs to
market?"

"Not for several weeks. They are still too wild for
that, Señor Fargo. They must be gentled more."

So much for that idea, thought Fargo. Maybe there
was another answer.

"If you don't mind my asking, why do you have
your herd over here and your family's camp on the
other side of the river?"

"This is the best place to keep the mesteños," Barrientos explained, using the Spanish word for wild
horses from which the more familiar mustang had been
derived. "In the morning you will see that there is a
small spring at the base of the bluff, so they have water,
and there is a little grass for them inside the corral.
The chaparral is nearby, which gives us the material
for the fence. But there is no other water closer than
the river. Since my family had to stay over there anyway, I found a place where they could be the most
comfortable."

"But split up that way, you have to leave somebody
over here all the time to guard the horses," Fargo
pointed out.

Barrientos shrugged again. "Until tonight, I believed the only thing that threatened our herd was
coyotes. The Comanches have not raided in this area

for almost ten years, and we are too far from the border to be troubled by bandidos. Until Johnny Lobo came along . . ."

"Where's he from?" Fargo asked. "I heard him yelling tonight, and he didn't sound Mexican."

"I do not know. Some of my people ride with him, it is true, but like you, I do not believe he is a *Mejicano*, though he speaks the language fluently. He has just as many gringo outlaws in his band."

"Well, wherever he's from, he's a threat," Fargo said. "You might be better off bringing your family over here. You could fill water barrels at the river and get by that way until you have the horses ready to drive to market. And you could all stand guard."

Barrientos sighed. "An excellent suggestion, Señor Fargo, though it will be harder on my wife. My girls have grown accustomed to the frontier life, but Juliana . . . ah, she will always miss the luxuries she grew up with and continued to enjoy as a grown woman."

"She's from Spain, isn't she?"

"*Sí.* Her father was a diplomat who came to Mexico City, bringing his family with him, when Juliana was fourteen. I met her a year or so later. I was a dashing young medical student, and she was the beautiful daughter of an ambassador. The love between us was meant to be. I courted her, and we were married when she was seventeen. Antonia was born the year that Texas won its independence from Mexico. Elena and Ramona came along later. We would have had more children, of course, but Juliana's health declined and she could not withstand another birth. Only in recent years has she begun to regain some of her strength, and I fear that this harsh land may yet sap it away from her."

It was a long speech, but like Rooster, Barrientos

35

was clearly a man who enjoyed talking. Fargo didn't mind listening, either. He liked the family and was glad to know more about them.

"I was thinking," he said. "If you move your camp over here, Rooster could stay with you, too, and help you guard the herd while I deliver that load of cotton to Corpus Christi for him. He might not be up to bouncing fifty or sixty miles on a wagon, but he could pull a trigger if he needed to."

Barrientos' teeth shone white in the moonlight as he smiled. "An excellent idea, Señor Fargo! With six of us here, behind that fence of thorns, we could fight off any attack by bandits."

"I could be back from Corpus in three or four days, too, and then I'd be glad to stay around until those mustangs have got all the green rubbed off them."

"*Bueno!* It is a rare trouble that does not bring some good with it as well. In this case, the attack by Johnny Lobo has also brought us your friendship, Señor Fargo."

"It's settled, then," Fargo said, returning the older man's smile. "All we've got to do is get Rooster to go along with it."

"There ain't nothin' wrong with me, dagnabbit! This here little scratch ain't bad enough to keep me from doin' my job!"

Rooster was being as contrary as Fargo had expected him to be. The old-timer stood beside the campfire, his back stiff from the bandages Barrientos had wound around his midsection.

"You said yourself that Señor Barrientos used to be a doctor, and a good one," Fargo pointed out. "He says you're not up to the trip. But I am, and I'm perfectly willing to deliver that cotton for you."

"I said he used to be a sawbones," Rooster grumbled. "Never said nothin' about him bein' a good one."

"It was implied," Fargo said dryly.

"Anyway," Rooster blustered, "how do I know you won't steal my wagon and that load o' cotton?"

"Señor Rooster!" Juliana Barrientos scolded. "Señor Fargo has proven to be a friend to all of us. One can tell by looking at him that he is not a thief."

"No, I reckon he ain't," Rooster admitted grudgingly. "Sorry, Fargo. Say, I been thinkin'. . . . That name, Skye Fargo, sounded familiar to me. It come to me last night. . . . You're the fella they call the Trailsman, ain't you?"

"Some do," Fargo said with a nod.

Elena was close enough to hear. She said, "What is this . . . Trailsman?"

Rooster pointed at Fargo. "Him. Done some scoutin' for the army, guided wagon trains across the prairie, fought Injuns and outlaws just about ever' place from the Rio Grande to the Milk River. From what I hear, he just can't seem to dodge trouble. It keeps findin' him, reg'lar as clockwork."

Fargo chuckled and said, "It does seem like that sometimes. But really, I'm just a peaceable man who likes to drift around and see the country."

"Well, you've seen a heap of it, from what I hear. But that ain't neither here nor there. How come you're tryin' to take over my job?"

"It's sort of my fault you've got that bullet hole in your side," Fargo said. "You told me that Johnny Lobo never bothered you before I came along. So the least I can do is see to it that your freight gets where it's supposed to go."

"Yeah, Lobo's been on more of a tear than usual,"

Rooster said. "He's got a burr up his backside for some reason." He nodded toward Juliana and Elena. "Beggin' your pardon for bein' crude about it, ladies."

Ramona was not in camp. She had ridden over to the mustang corral earlier in the morning, before Fargo returned to the Barrientos family's camp to propose his idea. When he had explained, the look in Juliana's eyes told him that she wasn't too fond of the prospect of leaving this comfortable camp to go to a place where both water and shade would be more scarce. But she was willing to do whatever her husband wanted and make the best of it.

Now it was just a matter of convincing Rooster to go along with the idea.

The old-timer started to stalk back and forth, but he stopped and winced as the motion pulled at the wound in his side. With a sigh, he said, "I reckon it would be a mite painful to have to wrestle with them mules and drive that wagon all the way to Corpus right now. You ever handled a team before, Fargo?"

"Many times," Fargo said with a nod.

"You know how to get to Corpus?"

"Follow the road, I expect."

Rooster nodded. "Yeah, it ain't all that hard. There's a little settlement down the road a ways called Dinero. They got a bridge where you cross the Nueces, and then the road follows the river right on down to Corpus. You can make it in two, two and a half days from here."

It sounded to Fargo like the old-timer was coming around to accepting the idea. He asked, "Where does the cotton go once I get there?"

"To a broker named Lucas Peabody. He's got a warehouse right on the waterfront. Corpus ain't as big a port as Indianola, up the coast a ways, or Brownsville, down at the mouth o' the Rio, but folks there are tryin' to build up the shippin' business. They do that by payin' better prices for goods goin' out, like cotton bound for the mills in England."

"So Peabody can be trusted?"

Rooster nodded. "Yep. I done business with him before. Deliver the cotton to him, and he'll give you the money to bring back to me."

"All right," Fargo said. He held out his hand. "Don't worry, Rooster. I won't let you down."

Rooster didn't hesitate. He clasped Fargo's hand and said, "That's good enough for me, comin' from an hombre like Skye Fargo."

Once the plans were agreed upon, it didn't take long to put them into action. Fargo helped Juliana and Elena pack up the camp, striking the tents and loading them onto the wagons along with the tables and chairs. When Fargo asked the two women if they could drive the wagons over to the mustang corral, they answered in the affirmative without hesitation.

"All of us have driven these wagons many miles," Elena said. "Do not worry about that, Señor Fargo."

"Why don't you call me Skye?" Fargo suggested.

Elena smiled. "I would like that." She glanced across the clearing at Juliana. "But I am not sure my mama would."

Fargo just grinned at her and went on with loading the family's goods onto the wagons.

Since it was possible that Johnny Lobo and his men were still roaming around the brush country, and might pose a problem even though it was broad daylight, Fargo planned to accompany the wagons to the corral and then return here for Rooster's wagon. When everything was loaded, he helped Rooster onto one of the wagon seats. The old man lowered himself gingerly to the seat. "I purely do hate bein' stove up like this," he complained.

"Then take care of yourself and you'll be getting around like normal that much quicker," Fargo said. Rooster just grumbled and scowled darkly.

It wasn't yet midmorning when they got under way. The trip went smoothly. Juliana and Elena handled the teams with ease, as they had claimed they could. They forded the Nueces, stopping long enough to fill all the water barrels on the wagons, and soon rolled into sight of the big corral set against the low sandy bluff. Fargo rode ahead of the wagons.

Antonia and Ramona sat on horseback with rifles resting across their saddles in front of them. Eduardo Barrientos had roped one of the mustangs and led it out of the big corral into a smaller enclosure that Fargo hadn't noticed the night before. In that smaller corral, Barrientos worked with the wild horse. He had it blindfolded and snubbed to a post in the center of the corral while he stood beside it and talked softly.

Antonia rode out to meet the newcomers. Fargo had left before dawn that morning, so now he got his first good look at her in full daylight. She was as lovely as he expected her to be, and the sight of her full red lips curving in a smile reminded him of how hot and sweet they had tasted the night before.

"Are you going to Corpus Christi, Señor Fargo?" she asked as she turned her horse and brought it alongside the Ovaro.

"That's right." Fargo smiled. "It took a little convincing to get Rooster to go along with the idea, but he came around." He added, as he had with Elena, "And why don't you call me Skye?"

"Of course . . . Skye. An unusual name, but it suits you." She paused and then went on, "I was thinking that perhaps I should accompany you to Corpus Christi since I have been over that trail many times."

"I reckon I can find my way all right. Besides, I don't think your father would go along with that."

Antonia's long hair was tucked up under her hat again. She gave a defiant toss of her head that threatened to dislodge the raven tresses. "My father, like all men from Mexico, thinks that women are fragile flowers to be protected and hidden away. Do I look fragile to you, Skye?"

He glanced over at her—tanned and limber, dressed in men's clothing and riding a horse like a man, with a rifle across her saddle and a six-gun on her hip.

"No, I don't reckon fragile describes you very well," he said. "But the flower part . . . well, I'd have to say you *are* as pretty as a flower."

She blushed, proving that frontier life hadn't drained all the femininity out of her.

"Unfortunately," Fargo went on, "you coming to Corpus with me is out of the question. I'm sorry, Antonia."

She gave another toss of her head as her mood changed instantly. "You should be," she said, and then she spurred ahead, leaving him to ponder what she meant by that.

Fargo slowed down and waited for the wagons. He rode up to the corral with them. Eduardo Barrientos left the mustang in the smaller corral and came out to greet them. He helped his wife down from the lead wagon and hugged her. "Now we are all together again," he said.

Juliana nodded, but Fargo didn't think she looked too enthusiastic about it. Well, to be fair, he thought, this place wasn't nearly as nice as their other camp had been. But it would do until they were ready to drive the mustangs to San Antonio.

He wanted to pick up Rooster's wagon and start on his journey to Corpus Christi as quickly as possible, but there were a few things he needed to discuss with Barrientos first. While the women helped Rooster down from the wagon and started to set up camp, Fargo drew Barrientos aside and spoke quietly to him.

"You'd better keep three people on guard at all times," Fargo said, "including one on top of that bluff. It's not very high, but it'll give whoever is up there a little better view of the countryside. If Lobo comes back, you'll have to make sure he doesn't try to send men around behind you. A couple of riflemen on the bluff could give you all the trouble you wanted."

Barrientos nodded. "*Sí*, Señor Fargo. This thought occurred to me as well. Fortunately, the chaparral is thick atop the bluff. It would be hard for men to work their way through it to attack us. Not impossible, but difficult, not to mention painful."

"I knew all those thorny mesquites were good for something," Fargo said with a smile.

"Do not worry, señor. We will be very watchful. If the Blessed Virgin smiles on us, there will be no trouble while you are gone. But if there is, we will meet it with stout hearts."

Fargo didn't doubt that for a second. He shook hands with Barrientos and then with Rooster. The girls looked like they wanted to hug him when he said good-bye to them, but they restrained themselves. Juliana just said, *"Vaya con Dios, Señor Fargo."*

He swung up onto the stallion, gave the family—and Rooster—a wave, and then rode back the way they had come.

When he reached the old campsite on the east side of the Nueces, he found the wagonload of cotton and the team of mules waiting for him, just as they had been left earlier in the day. Fargo hitched up the mules, tied the Ovaro's reins to the back of the wagon, and then climbed to the seat.

It had been a while since he'd worked as a teamster, but some things a fella never forgot. He picked up the reins, slapped them against the bony backs of the mules, and yelled at the stubborn beasts until they started moving.

To somebody who was used to the faster pace of a tireless stallion, driving a wagon behind a team of mules was incredibly slow. Fargo was glad he didn't have to make his living this way. The lure of the unknown had always called out to him, the desire to see what was on the other side of the next hill or around the next bend. At this rate, it would take forever to get there.

The miles gradually fell behind him, though. He had a full canteen and some frijoles and tortillas Señora Barrientos had prepared for him. At midday he stopped long enough to eat a little and let the mules rest. Then he pushed on southward. He thought he might reach that settlement Rooster had mentioned by nightfall.

Even though the sun was bright and the air was hot, Fargo knew that the heat would have been much worse during the summer. Texas weather was actually tolerable at certain times of year, and this was one of them.

He didn't encounter any other travelers during the afternoon. The brush country along the Nueces wasn't good for much. The land was too sandy for farming. A few men had started running cattle in here, but the grazing wasn't very good, either. Cows raised around here tended to be gaunt, rawboned critters with an incredibly wide sweep of horns. They were almost as wild as the mustangs that roamed the brasada.

The tiny settlement of Dinero existed because two

trails crossed there, the one from San Antonio to the Gulf Coast and another that ran between Goliad and Laredo. The bridge across the Nueces helped, too.

As the wagon approached the settlement late that afternoon, Fargo saw that it consisted of a single block of buildings that faced the river, along with a few houses scattered close by. The road turned and crossed the river just past that block. Most of the buildings were adobe, but there were a few frame structures as well.

At the north end of town stood a blacksmith's shop, and an adjoining corral and livery stable. At the south end was a church with a bell tower, its whitewashed adobe sides gleaming redly in the glow from the setting sun. Between the smithy and the church were a couple of stores, an adobe cantina, and the largest building in the settlement, a combined hotel and saloon made out of weathered planks. It even had a false front. Dinero wasn't much of a place, but it probably provided a welcome stopover for pilgrims on their way through this brushy wasteland.

A wagon was parked at one of the stores, and several horses were tied up at the hitch rail in front of the hotel and saloon, which evidently didn't have a name because its sign read simply HOTEL AND SALOON. The place had two entrances, one for each part of the business.

Fargo didn't intend to spend the night here, preferring to push on and camp somewhere south of the settlement, but he thought that it might be nice to have a beer and wash some of the trail dust from his throat. He headed the wagon toward the saloon.

He hadn't quite gotten there when the batwing doors at the saloon entrance suddenly slapped open and a man stumbled out in a hurry. The way he grabbed at the railing along the edge of the porch in an attempt to catch himself told Fargo that he hadn't left the saloon voluntarily.

Someone had thrown him out.

It wasn't any of Fargo's business, of course, but he pulled the mules to a halt as the man's grip slid off the railing and he toppled into the road, raising a little cloud of dust when he hit. Fargo didn't want the mules to step on the man, who might be drunk.

He didn't look drunk, though. As he rolled over, pushed himself onto his hands and knees, and swiveled his head to glance around wildly, he just looked scared.

He had good reason to be. Three men sauntered out of the saloon. Two were whites, roughly dressed in range clothes, the other a Mexican in charro garb, with little ornamental balls dangling from the wide brim of his sombrero. Fargo had always found that a somewhat silly affectation.

There was nothing silly about the ugly expression on the man's face, though, as he looked at the man in the street and said harshly, "You still here, hombre? I thought we told you to get the hell outta our sight."

"I . . . I'm going," the man in the street said as he got to his feet. "Right now, señor."

The Mexican reached for the fancy ivory handle of the gun on his hip. "I think maybe we should hurry you along." The white men laughed and joined him in drawing their pistols.

All three of them opened fire, spraying bullets around the feet of the man in the street. He leaped crazily into the air, bounding this way and that, trying to avoid the flying lead. A frightened, involuntary yell tore itself hoarsely from his throat.

Fargo watched the potentially deadly antics with a grim expression on his face. He didn't like bullies, and he especially didn't like it when their tormenting could seriously injure or even kill somebody. After a moment, he set the wagon's brake, jumped from the seat down to the street, and stepped up onto the porch.

The three men ignored him, but as their guns ran out of bullets and the racket of the shots died away, Fargo said in a loud, clear voice, "That's enough."

The Mexican turned his head to look at Fargo. The balls hanging from the brim of his sombrero swayed slightly as he said, "You talkin' to us, señor?"

"That's right."

The Mexican gestured with the barrel of his empty gun toward the man he and his companions had thrown out of the saloon, who was now hotfooting it down the road, taking advantage of the opportunity to get away. "That hombre is a friend of yours?"

"Never saw him before in my life," Fargo answered honestly.

"Then why do you wanna get mixed up in something that ain't none of your business, eh?"

"Because I don't like seeing a man have his heels nipped at by a pack of yapping curs," Fargo said flatly.

All three men stiffened angrily. One of the white men said, "Who the hell do you think you are, talkin' to us like that?"

"Doesn't matter who I am," Fargo said. "Any decent man would feel the same."

"They might feel it, señor," the Mexican said, "but they would have sense enough not to say it. You, on the other hand, are a damn fool." He patted his chest with the flat of his left hand. "You know who we are?"

"I think I already said," Fargo replied, an obvious reference to his earlier comment about yapping dogs.

The Mexican grinned. "Maybe you didn't notice . . . we already got guns in our hands. Yours is still in your holster."

Fargo smiled thinly and said, "Maybe *you* didn't

notice. All three of you emptied your guns. What do you think the odds are that I can kill all three of you before you can reload? Pretty good, I'd say."

He took a certain grim amusement from the expressions on the faces of the three men. First they looked startled by the realization that he was right, then a little fearful, then filled with rage. Common sense tempered that rage. They controlled themselves, even though it was difficult.

After a moment, the Mexican, who seemed to be the spokesman, said, "You got the upper hand right now, hombre, but it may not always be like this."

"I take things as they are, not how they might be," Fargo said.

"You remember our names, why don't you? I am Hector Rios, and these muchachos are Sanderson and DeWalt. We see you again sometime, eh?"

"Maybe. Question is, will I need eyes in the back of my head to see you?"

Hector Rios' swarthy face flushed even darker with anger. "First you call us dogs, and now you call us backshooters. You press your luck, señor. I speak for no one but myself when I say that if my lead finds you, you will see your death before you."

"Same here, mister," one of the other men grated out. The third man just nodded curtly.

"All right. Holster those hoglegs and move on."

Grudgingly, the three men slid their guns back into leather. They turned and walked away, from time to time casting resentful glances over their shoulders toward Fargo. They went to three of the horses tied at the hitch rail, unknotted the reins, and swung up onto their mounts. With spurts of dust puffing up from the hooves of the horses, Rios, Sanderson, and DeWalt rode away.

Fargo knew he had made enemies of the men. That

didn't bother him. He took it as something of a compliment that he had earned the enmity of cruel, cowardly lowlifes like that.

He turned back to the wagon, planning to tie the mules to the hitch rail and then go into the saloon to have that drink, but he stopped short when he saw who was sitting on horseback about ten yards away, a rifle held crossways across the saddle.

"Antonia," Fargo said, "what in blazes are you doing here?"

4

Antonia Barrientos wore a self-satisfied smile on her
lovely face. Holding the rifle in her left hand, she swung
down from the saddle and then walked toward Fargo,
leading the horse with her right. "I told you I ought to
go to Corpus Christi with you," she said. "Gone less
than a day and I come along and find you in trouble."

Fargo was annoyed with himself for not hearing Antonia ride up. His attention had been focused on the
three gunmen, but that was no excuse.

"That wasn't trouble," he said. "Their guns were
empty."

"Still, three of them, one of you," Antonia said as
she tied up the horse. She stepped up on the porch.
"One of them could have had another gun, or they
might have all pulled knives and jumped you. You
would have had a hard time getting all three of them.
That's why I was ready to help if I needed to."

Fargo decided he might as well be gracious about
it. "I'm obliged," he said. "That doesn't explain why

you're not still up at the mustang camp with the rest of your family."

"Doesn't it?" she said, and her smile was even more smug now.

"I reckon I see," Fargo said. "You're used to getting your own way."

Antonia shrugged.

"Which makes you a spoiled brat," Fargo went on.

The smile went away and she glared at him. "You could at least say you're glad to see me."

Fargo was about to respond that he *wasn't* glad to see her, but he realized that would have been a lie. Before he could say anything, however, a man spoke from the entrance of the saloon.

"Hey, mister."

Fargo didn't hear any menace in the words, so he turned easily, not tensed for trouble. The man in the doorway had pushed the batwings open and stood there with one hand on each of the swinging sections of door. He wore a gray shirt that had probably started out that way and a gray apron that had once been white, more than likely. He was tall and broad, but soft-looking, with thinning sandy hair and a long mustache that curled up on each end.

"You know who those hombres were?" he went on.

"Rios, Sanderson, and DeWalt," Fargo said. "Names don't mean a damned thing to me, but that's who the fella claimed they were."

The bartender, who might also be the owner of the saloon for all Fargo knew, said, "They're bad men. Some folks say they ride with Johnny Lobo. I've even heard rumors that Hector Rios is Lobo's segundo."

Fargo thought back to the previous day. He didn't recall seeing any of the three men with Lobo, but he hadn't had all that much time to study the members of the gang as they were trying to kill him. Sanderson and DeWalt were common hardcases, too, not really the type to stand out.

"You're lucky they didn't kill you," the bartender said. "You interfered with their fun."

"It didn't look like much fun for the man they were shooting at. Who was he?"

"His name's Alex Wilson. Owns one of the stores here in town. He was just standing at the bar, having a beer before he went home, when Rios and the others came in and started hoorawin' him. Alex is no gunnie. He couldn't fight back against that bunch."

Antonia had stepped up beside Fargo. She nudged him with an elbow and said, "It sounds like this Señor Wilson was lucky the Trailsman came along, doesn't it?"

The bartender's pale blue eyes widened as he looked at Fargo. "You're the Trailsman?"

"Some call me that," Fargo said. It would have been all right with him if Antonia hadn't mentioned it. Only rarely was his reputation a problem, such as when someone tried to pick a fight with him because of it. More often it came in handy, because people tended to take his words more seriously. But really, Fargo didn't think a lot about it either way.

"Well, then, maybe Rios and the other two are the lucky ones. Come on in and have a drink, Mr. Fargo. On the house."

Fargo wasn't going to decline that offer. He turned to Antonia and said, "As long as you're here, I guess you can keep an eye on the cotton while I'm inside."

"Nobody's going to bother that cotton," she said. "I thought I'd have a drink, too."

"Saloon's no place for a lady," Fargo said.

Antonia snorted. "Good thing I'm not one, then. Disappointing your mama and papa comes in handy every now and then, I suppose."

Fargo wasn't going to waste time and energy arguing with her. More than twenty-four hours had passed since Johnny Lobo and the other outlaws had jumped him in the chaparral. Many of those hours had been eventful ones, and relatively few of them had been spent in sleep. He wanted that drink, and then he was going to push on.

The question was whether or not he would be able to persuade Antonia not to accompany him.

And did he really want her to go back to the mustang camp?

They went into the saloon, where the bartender introduced himself as Jack Hagen. He was indeed the proprietor of the place, running the saloon half of the business while his wife Eula looked after the hotel part. He drew a beer for Fargo, then looked dubiously at Antonia as he said, "I don't reckon I've got anything fittin', like sarsaparilla, for a young woman to drink, señorita."

"Give me tequila, then," Antonia said.

Hagen looked at Fargo, who shrugged. It was Antonia's business what sort of firewater she poured down her gullet.

Hagen poured the drink. Antonia picked up the glass, threw back the tequila, and gasped. A shudder ran through her. Her hand shook a little as she put the glass back on the bar. "Good," she said hoarsely.

"Want another?" Fargo asked mildly.

Antonia shook her head. "That's enough."

Fargo drank from his beer to conceal the smile that played briefly across his face. Antonia wasn't as tough and worldly as she was trying to act. She was a far cry from the typical demure young Mexican woman, true enough, but some of her behavior was just a facade.

"Are you going to spend the night here?" she asked.

Fargo shook his head. "No, I thought I'd push on a little farther down the trail and camp somewhere."

Hagen said, "Excuse me for buttin' in, Mr. Fargo, but the beds in the hotel are a whole heap more comfortable than a bedroll on a patch of hard ground somewhere. A little less likely that a scorpion or some other varmint will crawl in your blankets here, too."

Fargo thought it over quickly. The day was too far gone for Antonia to start back to her family's camp until the next morning. And since his brief stay in Dinero had already turned out to be longer than he had expected, he couldn't really get very far down the trail to Corpus Christi before having to stop again. It made more sense to just stay here.

"All right," he said, "but I expect to pay for my room, and for any more drinks or food."

Hagen grinned. "Deal. My wife wouldn't let me offer you a room on the house, anyway. She's got all the business sense in the family." He looked at Antonia. "And you'll be staying the night, too, señorita?"

"*Sí,*" Antonia said. She reached into a pocket of her denim trousers. "I have money. . . ."

Fargo put out a hand to stop her. "I'll take care of it," he said.

A fiercely proud look came onto Antonia's face. "I am still a Barrientos," she declared. "I can pay my own way."

"Yeah, but the only reason you rode down here was to keep me out of trouble, right? The least I can do is pay for your hotel room. Besides, I got lucky in a poker game in San Antonio, so I've got a pretty good stake."

She frowned in thought for a moment, then sighed. "All right, Skye. I am grateful."

"No need." Fargo took out a buckskin poke and

extracted a couple of coins. As he slid them across the hardwood to Hagen, he went on. "That ought to cover the room and supper for both of us."

"Yes, sir," Hagen said as he deftly made the money disappear. "That'll be just fine. And we'll throw in feed for your horses and your team, too. Corral's around back. Just go right through there"—he nodded toward an arched doorway that connected the saloon to the hotel lobby—"and my wife will fix you right up. Just tell her that you made the arrangements with me."

"Obliged," Fargo said. He started toward the hotel lobby. Antonia fell in step beside him.

He had a feeling that, come morning, she might prove difficult to get rid of. Not that he didn't enjoy her company, but all the reasons he'd had for not letting her come along on this journey in the first place were still valid.

He would deal with that when the time came, he told himself. For now he just wanted something to eat, followed by a good night's sleep.

Eula Hagen was a tiny birdlike woman, and Fargo wondered why women like that often wound up with big galoots like her husband. They seemed to be a pretty good match, though—she was brisk and business-like, while Hagen was more easygoing and friendly. They had turned their hotel and saloon into a going concern in this little crossroads settlement, so they had to be doing something right.

The hotel had a small dining room on the other side of the lobby from the saloon. Fargo and Antonia had supper there after registering and tending to the horses and mules. Fargo thought it was unlikely any-body would bother the load of cotton while it was parked in the hotel's corral.

The meal consisted of strips of beef fried with peppers and onions, along with tortillas in which the meat was rolled, and of course plenty of frijoles. Fargo figured the beef came from one of those long-horned cows that roamed the brush country, because it was tough and stringy, but overall the food was pretty good. He was satisfied, anyway, when he and Antonia finished.

"What are you going to do now?" she asked.

"Sleep. I plan to be back on the trail at first light. The sooner I get to Corpus and deliver that cotton for Rooster, the sooner I can get back up to the camp to lend a hand if you and your family need it."

"You talk like I'm going to be there waiting for you," Antonia said. "I told you, Skye, I'm going with you."

"Not a good idea."

"Oh? Is it better to send me back through the brasada by myself while Johnny Lobo and his men are roaming around?"

Fargo frowned. That very concern had been lurking in the back of his mind, but now that Antonia had given voice to it, it couldn't be ignored. She had been lucky that no one had bothered her while she was riding alone, catching up to him. She might not be so fortunate if she set out on her own again.

"We'll figure it out in the morning," he said. From the smile that passed across Antonia's face, he knew she thought that she had won.

The hotel rooms were on either side of a hallway that ran straight back from the lobby, four on each side. Mrs. Hagen had put Fargo in the farthest room on the left side, while Antonia was closest to the lobby on the right. Fargo didn't figure it was an accident that they were as far apart as possible. It was already scandalous enough for a young woman to be staying in a hotel room with no chaperone.

Fargo said good night to Antonia at her door. He went on to his room, where he had left his saddlebags and his Henry rifle earlier. The room was small, barely eight feet wide, and most of the space was taken up by the bed. There was a single narrow window, open to let in the night breezes.

Fargo leaned the Henry in a corner, moved his saddlebags from the bed to the floor, and undressed by the light of a single candle that sat on a tiny table next to the bed. The night was warm, so after he blew out the candle he sprawled on top of the sheets, not wanting any cover.

Even though he was tired, his senses remained alert. He took stock of the night sounds that drifted through the window, along with the faint breeze, and didn't hear anything out of the ordinary. Relaxing, he dozed off, although long habit ensured that a part of his brain remained on a hair trigger.

It was that instinct, conditioned by years of danger, that warned him a couple of hours later when someone came in through the window.

All it took was an extra rustle of the curtain, the whisper of a foot on the floor, to bring Fargo wide awake instantly. His senses operated at peak efficiency. Silently, his right arm moved and his hand closed over the butt of his Colt, which hung in its holster from the headboard of the bed. The noise of metal sliding out of oiled leather wasn't audible more than six inches away.

Fargo sat up, his thumb on the revolver's hammer. His keen eyes saw a dark shape looming in front of the window.

The smart thing would be to start blasting before the intruder knew that Fargo was aware of his presence. But Fargo held his fire, unwilling to kill somebody without knowing who it was. The thought that

Rios or one of the other gunnies might have come back to even the score with him hammered in his brain.

But the scent that his keen sense of smell suddenly picked up didn't come from some trail-dust-covered gunman with horseshit on his boots. What Fargo smelled was clean female flesh and long, thick hair, and even in the darkness of this room he knew that hair was as black as a raven's wing. . . .

"Damn it, Antonia," he said as he lowered the gun, "do you have any idea how close I just came to shooting you?"

She gasped, and he heard her jump back as well, surprised not only that he was awake but also that he knew perfectly well who had just climbed through the window into his room. "Skye," she said.

He swung his legs off the bed and stood up, stepping toward her. He bumped against her in the darkness, and his left arm went around her, pulling her tighter to him. She wore a thin shift of some sort, but from the feel of her firm flesh under his touch, that was all.

"What are you doing here?" he asked her.

"I . . . I wanted to be with you. That room, it is lonely."

"Why didn't you just come down the hall and knock on the door?"

Antonia sniffed. "And let that little biddy of a hotel keeper know what I was doing? I climbed out my window and went around behind the corral to reach your room. My business is my own, Skye." She ran her hands over his broad, muscular chest. "And I see nothing wrong with observing a *few* of the proprieties. . . ."

"Just not all of them, eh?"

"No," she whispered as her hands strayed lower

57

and discovered the fact that he was nude. "Not all of them."

She leaned against him, and when he lowered his face to hers, their lips found each other unerringly despite the darkness. The heated kiss was urgent. Fargo felt desire rise in him, and Antonia felt it, too, as his stiffening shaft prodded the softness of her belly.

Reaching down, she tried to close the fingers of one hand around the long, thick pole, only to realize that one hand wasn't enough to go around it. *"Dios mio,"* she whispered. "Skye, I had no idea. . . ."

"Want to leave?" he asked dryly.

"Are you a madman? Leaving is the last thing I want to do!"

Fargo kissed her some more and ran a hand over her body, pausing to cup each firm breast in turn. He felt her hard nipples through the thin fabric of her shift. Breaking the kiss, she said breathlessly, "I . . . I want to be naked. There must be nothing between us."

"Wait a minute," Fargo said.

Moving to the small table beside the bed, he felt around until he found a block of sulfur matches. He snapped one of the lucifers to life with his thumbnail and held the flame to the candlewick. It caught and grew stronger, sending its soft, inconstant yellow glow through the room. Fargo turned to Antonia and said, "I wanted to see you. Now you can get undressed."

She smiled as she reached down to the hem of her shift and peeled it up and over her head. Her thick black hair tangled in the garment for a second before she pulled it loose, so she had to give her head a shake to straighten her hair. The unself-conscious gesture made her even more beautiful.

She was all sleek, honey-colored skin and dark brown nipples and curves sweeping sensuously in and out and a triangle of black, finespun hair at the juncture of her thighs. Fargo stepped over to her and took her in his arms again. As he kissed her, he reached down and cupped that triangle of hair, pressing the ball of his hand against the mound that it covered. Instinctively, Antonia's legs parted slightly as Fargo caressed her.

He felt hot dampness against his fingers as he explored between her thighs. She moaned against his mouth and moved her hips slightly. His middle finger slid over her slickness and slipped into her, penetrating her core. Antonia hunched harder against his hand.

However, she wasn't so consumed by pleasure that she had forgotten about him. She grasped his manhood with both hands this time and pumped them up and down the shaft. Under her tender touch, Fargo grew rock hard, and he knew the passion mounting inside him wasn't going to be denied for long.

He took his finger out of Antonia, causing her to make a little sound of loss, but he steered her quickly to the bed and laid her down on it. She spread her legs wide in invitation. Fargo wanted to sheathe himself inside her right away, but he controlled the urge long enough to kneel between her thighs and lower his head to her sex. He spread the folds with his thumbs and plunged his tongue into her. She cried out in ecstasy and her hips gave a little bounce off the bed. For a moment she wrapped her legs around his head, the muscular thighs pressing against his ears, trapping him there—not that he minded.

A spasm ran through her as his tongue delved inside her. Then her muscles relaxed and her head sagged back on the pillow, her eyes closing. Fargo lifted himself and was content for a moment to watch her beautiful breasts rising and falling rapidly as she tried to catch her breath. His member was still like a bar of iron, though, so he wasn't through with her yet. Not by a long shot.

Her legs were parted again. Fargo positioned himself between them and brought the head of his shaft to her drenched opening. With a powerful thrust of his hips, he drove it into her. That made her eyes pop open again, and her mouth formed an O of excitement and pleasure. "Skye!" she breathed. "So big . . . so big . . ."

He plunged in and out of her, each stroke taking him deep inside her. Antonia met his thrusts with her own, pumping her hips up and down and giving as good as she got. Fargo felt his arousal growing stronger and stronger until culmination burst on him and he drove into her one final time. He held himself there, buried as deep as he could go in her, and emptied himself into her in a scalding, throbbing explosion.

The long, slow slide down the other side of the peak left him limp and satiated. As he rested on top of her for a moment, she slipped her arms around him and hugged him tightly. "That was so good, Skye," she whispered in his ear. "So good . . ."

He could have stayed right there, but he didn't want his weight crushing her. He rolled off and then stretched out beside her, slipping his arms around her and cuddling her to him. The clean scent of her hair filled his senses as she rested her head on his chest. Idly, he stroked a hand down the smooth sweep of her back to the sweet, swelling fullness of her hips.

Both of them dozed off that way, still sharing the closeness they had experienced.

Fargo wasn't sure at first what woke him, but then he sniffed the air and knew.

Smoke.

Few things were more feared on the frontier than fire. A blaze could leap from building to building and burn an entire town to the ground. If the flames spread to the prairie—or in this case, the brushy, mostly dry expanse of the South Texas brasada—they might roar across the countryside and consume millions of acres. Nothing was more devastating than a wildfire.

Fargo flung himself out of bed and grabbed for his clothes. Behind him, Antonia gasped in surprise as Fargo's sudden movement startled her out of sleep. "Skye, what is it?" she asked.

"Get up and get dressed quick as you can," Fargo told her. "Something's burning."

Antonia sniffed the air and exclaimed in Spanish as she smelled the pungent smoke, too. She sprang up and grabbed her shift, which was the only garment she had with her. "Everything in my room—" she began.

Fargo stomped his feet down into his boots and clapped his hat on his head. "Stick close to me," he said as he buckled on his gun belt. Then he picked up his saddlebags and the Henry rifle.

Going to the door, he opened it slightly. The hotel was quiet. No one was in the corridor. It appeared that Fargo was the first one to notice the smoke.

Antonia crowded close behind him. He opened the door wider and told her, "Hurry down to your room and grab your gear. It's about to be so hectic around here that nobody will think twice about where you were before all hell broke loose."

With that he threw open the door and stepped into the hall. Antonia ran past him, heading for her room. Fargo didn't know how many of the other rooms in the hotel were occupied, but he stopped at all of them just in case, pounding on them with the flat of his hand and shouting, "Fire! Fire!"

Doors were jerked open behind him as he went up the hall toward the front of the hotel. By the time he reached Antonia's door she came back out into the hall, wearing trousers and a shirt now—although the shirt hung open over the shift underneath it—and with her hat crammed on her head. She carried her rifle and boots. Fargo pressed his saddlebags and rifle into her hands, too.

"Out the front," Fargo told her. He looked over his shoulder and saw that three men, traveling salesmen from the look of them, had emerged from the other rooms. He waved the drummers on and told them, "Get out of the building! The place may be on fire!"

So far he hadn't see any flames, but the smoke seemed to be getting thicker. Once he was sure all the rooms were empty and the guests had all fled, he moved into the lobby.

At that moment, with a huge *whoosh*, flames exploded through the arched opening between the hotel and the saloon. It was the saloon that was on fire, Fargo realized, but the place was all one big building, so the hotel was doomed. The fire had reached the liquor supply in the saloon and was now burning fiercely.

Heat pounded at Fargo's face as he turned toward the inferno. "Hagen!" he shouted. "Hagen, are you still in here?"

He wasn't sure where the couple had their quarters. The hour was late enough that the saloon was probably closed and both Jack and Eula Hagen had turned in for the night. As the flames began to spread along the wall behind the registration desk, Fargo hurried over to the hotel entrance and looked out into the street, searching for any sign of the Hagens. He didn't see them among the rapidly gathering crowd. A few men were trying to form a bucket brigade stretching from the Nueces River to the hotel, but Fargo knew that effort was doomed. The fire was too far along for it to do any good.

He couldn't go into the saloon to look for Hagen; that would be like stepping into the very bowels of Hell. Fargo coughed as the thick, choking smoke clawed at his nose and throat. He couldn't stay in here much longer.

"H-help! Somebody help me!"

The faint cry came from the dining room. Fargo turned toward it and saw Eula Hagen trying to haul the limp bulk of her much bigger husband through the door. Their living quarters had to be somewhere behind the dining room, Fargo realized. He didn't know what had happened to Jack Hagen, but the man seemed to be unconscious. And Eula was too small to do more than barely budge him.

Fargo ran over to her and said over the crackling roar of the flames, "I'll get him! Go out the front!"

"No, I'll help you!" she cried. "If we can just get him on his feet—"

Fargo bent, got his hands under Hagen's arms, and lifted. The saloon keeper was four or five inches taller than Fargo and probably outweighed him by fifty or sixty pounds. Fargo grunted with the effort as he tried to haul Hagen upright. Eula grabbed her husband and helped as much as she could, but she didn't have much strength.

Hagen finally came up onto his feet. He wasn't completely dead weight now, but he was still only half conscious and didn't seem to have any idea of what was going on. In the flickering glare of the flames that lit the hotel lobby brightly, Fargo saw a large, bloody welt on the man's head and knew that somebody had clouted the hell out of him. That meant this blaze probably wasn't accidental, something that Fargo's gut already had him suspecting.

With Fargo on one side taking most of the weight and Eula on the other steadying her husband, they steered Hagen toward the door. Between the heat and the effort, Fargo was drenched with sweat. He was closer to the flames, and the intensity of them seared his lungs and made it hard to breathe, as did the smoke that coiled around them. After what seemed like an eternity of trying to cross the hotel lobby, they finally reached the door and stumbled out onto the porch. The air was a little fresher here, enough so that it seemed like cool wine to Fargo.

Several dozen people were in the street. Some of the men sprang forward to take hold of Jack Hagen and relieve Fargo of the burden. Others were still futilely flinging buckets of water on the hotel and saloon.

"Forget about this building!" Fargo rasped at them, raising his voice to be heard over the roaring flames. "Wet down the other buildings! Keep the fire from spreading!"

Now that everybody seemed to be safe, he remembered the horses and mules in the corral behind the hotel, not to mention the wagonload of cotton. He thought the corral was big enough that the animals could stay back from the flames and survive. If enough sparks fell on the wagon, though, they might set it and its contents afire. Fargo turned sharply, thinking that he had to get back there and see what the situation was.

The move saved his life, because at that instant he felt the wind-rip of a bullet's passage only inches from his ear and knew that somebody had just tried to kill him.

5

Fargo's hand flashed to the Colt on his hip. Out of the corner of his eye he had caught the flash of a gun muzzle in the thick shadows of the alley at the side of the hotel. As he dropped to one knee and drew the revolver, orange flame spouted again in the alley. Fargo brought up the Colt and thumbed off two fast shots. Their thunder was almost lost in the commotion.

He saw another muzzle flash, but this one was directed upward, telling him that the shot had been loosed as whoever was wielding the gun fell over. Fargo surged upright and ran toward the alley, confident that he had hit whoever had tried to ambush him.

Thoughts raced through his head. If somebody wanted to kill him, what better way to force him out into the open than to set fire to the hotel? Of course, the blaze could have killed a lot of other people, too, but the bushwhacker didn't care about that.

Knowing that the man in the alley might just be

wounded, Fargo veered suddenly toward the hotel and bounded up onto the porch so that he could place his back against the front wall. He felt the heat through the boards and knew it wouldn't be long before this part of the building was burning, too, but for the moment the flames hadn't reached this far. They were crawling along the roof above the porch, though, heading in his direction. He didn't have much time.

Crouching low, with the Colt held ready to fire, Fargo went swiftly around the corner of the building into the alley. His foot kicked something yielding, and he dropped to a knee. He reached out with his left hand and found a body lying on its back. The man's chest was wet and sticky with blood. Fargo ran his hand on up to the bushwhacker's throat. There was no pulse. The man was dead.

Under the circumstances, Fargo's shots had been near miraculous. At least one of the bullets had struck the bushwhacker in the chest and killed him. Fargo leaned closer, but he couldn't see who the man was. The nearby flames actually made the alley darker than it usually was, because they strengthened the shadow cast by the building.

Fargo figured he could narrow down the man's identity anyway. The bushwhacker was probably one of the three hardcases he had confronted the day before. The man had come back to take revenge for being run out of Dinero at gunpoint.

And if one of them could come back to settle the score, so could another—

That thought went through Fargo's mind just as a heavy weight slammed into his back and knocked him forward. His hat came off, and fingers grabbed his hair and jerked his head back painfully. Fargo knew what would come next—the sweep of a knife blade across his throat, the hot red gush of blood, the darkness of death closing in on him. . . .

But not if he could do anything about it. With all the blinding speed he could muster, guided by his instincts, he brought his gun up in front of his throat. Metal clashed on metal as the knife blade hit the barrel of the Colt instead of biting deep into Fargo's neck. Fargo heaved himself up, arching his back, and the attacker was thrown off. Fargo rolled in what he hoped was the opposite direction.

He wound up on his belly, near the end of the hotel porch. The roof over the porch collapsed at that moment, and some of the sparks and bits of burning debris showered down around Fargo, stinging painfully everywhere they hit bare skin. The fiery collapse sent enough of a reflected glow into the alley, however, so that he could make out the form of the man lunging at him, knife upraised for a killing stroke.

Fargo tipped up the barrel of the Colt and squeezed off a shot. The bullet hit his attacker under the chin and bored at an upward angle through the man's brain, flipping him over backward as it killed him.

There had been three of the hardcases, Fargo reminded himself as he scrambled to his feet. The other one could still be lurking around somewhere. But the wall of the hotel next to the alley was on fire now, and Fargo could see well enough by the light of the flames to know that the alley was empty. He holstered his Colt and hurried forward to grab the collars of both of the dead men. He wanted to be sure who they were, so he dragged them into the street where the fire shouldn't be able to reach them.

Then he ran back along the alley, bent again on his original errand to check on the livestock behind the hotel.

The Ovaro, Antonia's horse, and Rooster's mules were the only animals in the corral. Fargo swung the gate open so they could get out if they needed to. Then he hurried to the wagon parked near the rear wall of the hotel and lifted the singletree, propping it against the seat. After disengaging the brake lever, Fargo went behind the wagon and put his shoulder against the tailgate. He wanted to roll the vehicle farther away from the building.

The wagon was heavy to start with, and with its load of cotton adding to the weight, Fargo couldn't make it move no matter how hard he grunted and strained. Then, suddenly, a big shape was beside him, and Jack Hagen called, "Lemme give you a hand!" Blood dripped down his face from the gash on his head.

With both of them pushing, the wagon began to move. Several other men ran up and added their strength to the task, and within seconds they had the wagon rolling easily. They didn't stop pushing until the wagon was well past the back of the corral. It gradually came to a stop.

His chest heaving from the exertion, Fargo turned and looked at the hotel and saloon. The whole building was ablaze now, the flames leaping high into the night from the burning roof. A part of the roof fell in, sending a huge shower of sparks spiraling into the black sky.

Fargo looked over at Jack Hagen, who didn't seem too steady on his feet. "Are you all right?" Fargo asked hoarsely.

"Still dizzy as hell," Hagen answered, "but Eula said you saved my life—and probably hers, too, because she wouldn't have left me—so when I saw you come back here I thought I'd better lend a hand with whatever you came to do."

"And we just followed Jack, mister," one of the other men said. "Didn't want anything to happen to him. Figured he'd had enough bad luck for one night."

"Luck didn't have anything to do with it," Fargo said grimly. "That fire was set. Come on."

Picking up his hat along the way, he led the way back to the road that formed Dinero's only real street. Waving a hand at the two bodies, Fargo went on, "Those are the two bastards responsible for this."

"Say, I'm startin' to remember now!" Hagen said as he wiped some of the blood from his face. "I had closed up the saloon when I thought I heard something outside, so I went to check. I saw a couple of fellas in the alley on the other side of the building and smelled coal oil. They were fixin' to start that fire!"

"That's right," Fargo said. "What happened then?"

"Well, I let out a yell and they jumped me." Hagen sounded vaguely embarrassed as he went on, "I'm a big son of a gun, but I ain't much of a fighter, if you know what I mean. One of 'em clouted me with a gun butt or somethin'. That's all I remember until I woke up inside the saloon and the place was on fire."

Fargo nodded. "They must have carried you inside, thinking that you'd be killed in the fire. That way nobody would know they'd attacked you and started the blaze."

Hagen rubbed his jaw and said, "Yeah, I reckon. When I came to, I knew I had to get Eula outta there. She'd already gone to bed, so I headed for our room. I remember gettin' there, but then . . . nothin'. I must've passed out again from gettin' walloped on the head."

That made sense to Fargo. He knew the rest of it.

Except for the identities of the two arsonists and would-be killers. He walked over to the corpses and looked down at them, recognizing the rough-hewn, beard-stubbled faces in the light from the flames.

Sanderson and DeWalt.

"They said they weren't backshooters," Fargo mused. "Reckon they were liars, to boot."

Antonia had been part of the crowd watching the conflagration. Now she spotted Fargo and hurried over to him, throwing her arms around him when she reached him. "Skye!" she said. "Are you all right?"

Fargo smiled tiredly. "A little singed around the edges, but nothing to worry about. How about you?"

"I'm fine. I just . . . I just looked around and I didn't see you, and I was afraid something might have happened to you."

"Something almost did, and it wasn't for lack of trying on their part," Fargo said with a nod toward the bodies of Sanderson and DeWalt. Antonia looked at them and shuddered.

"Johnny Lobo's men," she said.

"Yeah, but I reckon they weren't following Lobo's orders this time. This was some personal hell-raising on their part. They wanted to get back at me for what happened yesterday."

One of the townspeople had come up to listen to what Fargo was saying, and now he spoke up. "Mr. Fargo, I . . . I feel like this is all my fault."

Fargo looked at him with a puzzled frown. The man's face was a little familiar, but it took Fargo a second to place him. "You're Alex Wilson, aren't you?"

The man nodded. "That's right. I own the store over there." He pointed to one of the buildings north of the burning saloon and hotel. "It was because of me that you had to step in and make enemies of those men in the first place. I'm to blame for the Hagens' place burning down, and it could have cost a lot of people their lives."

With one arm still around Antonia, Fargo faced the

man and said, "Let me tell you something, Mr. Wilson. When a cowardly bully tries to run roughshod over somebody, it's sure as hell not the fault of the fella who was unlucky enough to be in his way. It's the bully's fault and nobody else's, and whatever happens is on his head. The real reason those two set fire to the hotel, clouted Hagen, and tried to kill me is because they were evil bastards. What happened to them, they had coming. Simple as that."

Wilson nodded and looked as if Fargo's words had eased his mind somewhat.

The fire was beginning to burn itself out. The townspeople had wet down the surrounding buildings with river water and had been alert in dousing any falling embers that had landed in dangerous spots. The hotel and saloon building was going to be a total loss, though. Jack and Eula Hagen stood watching the blaze and holding each other. They were obviously glad to still be alive, but they also looked stricken by their loss.

Alex Wilson went over to them and reached up to put a hand on big Jack Hagen's shoulder. "Don't worry, Jack," he said. "We'll help you rebuild. I'm sure the whole town will pitch in. We'll have a new building up in no time."

Several people in the crowd spoke up in agreement, creating a chorus of encouragement and support for the Hagens. Fargo knew they would follow through on their promises. A man like Alex Wilson might not be able to stand up to a bunch of gunmen, but he was a good friend and neighbor, and wouldn't let the Hagens down.

"Skye, what are we going to do?" Antonia asked.

"Well, once the fire's died down so that it's not a danger anymore, I intend to bed down under Rooster's wagon and try to get some sleep. Tomorrow morning I'll be pushing on to Corpus Christi with that cotton."

"You think that there is . . . room for one more under that wagon?"

Fargo smiled down at her and said, "I expect there is."

By morning the fire was completely burned out, leaving the hotel and saloon nothing but a pile of ashes and a heap of charred timbers. People got to work right away, though, at clearing away the debris so the place could be rebuilt.

There was no undertaker in Dinero, but the padre down at the church, Father Pascual, had taken charge of the bodies of Sanderson and DeWalt. He told Fargo that he would see to it that they received a proper burial, even though they had ridden with that great evildoer, Johnny Lobo.

"You know anything about him, Padre?" Fargo asked as he and Antonia stood in front of the church with the priest. The wagon full of cotton was there, too, with the mule team hitched to it, and the stallion and Antonia's horse tied on behind.

Father Pascual was a small, mostly bald man with the sad, determined eyes of one who has seen too much pain and suffering in the world but remains strong in his faith anyway. He said, "It is strange that you ask me that, my son. There is no doubt of Johnny Lobo's sins. He has murdered and stolen in front of many witnesses, and laughed at the monstrousness of his deeds. And yet . . . and yet one night, when I was alone in the church at my prayers, I heard the heavy tread of someone coming in, and when I arose and looked around, it was none other than he. In the light of the candles, the evil he has done was etched on his face. But he had in his hand a bag of soft buckskin, and when he held it out to me, what was inside it clinked like music. Coins, my son. Gold coins. Not a fortune, but a considerable amount. Enough to help feed the poor of the brasada for a good long time."

Enthralled by the story, Antonia said quietly, "Surely you did not take them, Padre. Money so stained with blood can bring nothing with it but misfortune!"

Father Pascual smiled. "That was my first thought as well, child, and it must have shown on my face because Johnny Lobo said to me, 'You are wrong, Padre. No blood stains these coins. They were earned honestly, many years ago, and I have been waiting all those years for the right place to leave them. My heart tells me this is the place.' "

"Doesn't sound like the usual owlhoot," Fargo commented with a slight frown.

"No, at that moment, he was both less . . . and more," Father Pascual agreed. He reached into a pocket of his robe. "I kept back one of the coins, though I used the others as he wished, to help feed the poor. Here it is."

He held out a gold coin. Fargo took it, feeling the weight of it, and turned it over in his fingers. Antonia leaned in to take a look at the coin, too. "A Spanish doubloon," she said. "It's very old."

"Like something from a pirate's booty," Fargo said. He handed the coin back to Father Pascual.

"I keep it," the padre said, "to remind myself that even in the most tainted of souls, there may yet be found a ray of light."

"I wouldn't want to risk my life on any light that might be found in Johnny Lobo's soul."

Father Pascual sighed. "You are right about that, my son. Sooner or later, all candles . . . go out."

Fargo and Antonia had already said their good-byes

to the Hagens, Alex Wilson, and the other citizens of Dinero. Now they said farewell to Father Pascual and climbed up onto the wagon seat. Fargo took up the reins and got the team moving.

As he drove across the bridge that spanned the Nueces River, he said, "Don't think you won just because you talked me into letting you come along. You still should have stayed up at the camp with your family."

Antonia smiled. "Yes, but once I was here, it was too dangerous to send me back alone, no?"

"That's right. But when we get back, if your papa decides you ought to be paddled like the rebellious child you are, don't expect me to step in and stop him."

Antonia tossed her head defiantly. "I am no child, Skye Fargo! You should know that better than anyone."

Fargo couldn't help but chuckle a little. "Yeah, I reckon you're right about that." After they had ridden along for a few minutes in silence, he went on, "You at least left your folks a note so they'd know where you went, didn't you?"

"Of course. I did not wish for them to worry."

"Oh, I imagine they're worried about you," Fargo said. "They don't have any way of knowing that you caught up to me, or whether or not you're safe. I expect they all did a lot of worrying last night."

Antonia frowned, as if in her impulsiveness she hadn't thought about that result of her actions. After a moment she said quietly, "Perhaps I deserve that paddling after all."

Fargo just clicked his tongue at the mules and flapped the reins.

They drove on south toward Corpus Christi all day, pausing only occasionally. By the middle of the day,

Fargo began to taste salt on his lips and knew it came from the gulf, carried northward by the prevailing southerly winds. That was a sure sign they were nearing the coast and ought to reach Corpus the next day.

They camped that night in some cottonwoods, a short distance off the road. Fargo had been keeping an eye on their backtrail all day, just in case Hector Rios might be following them, looking for revenge as Sanderson and DeWalt had done. Even though there had been no sign of trouble since leaving Dinero, Fargo decided they would have a cold camp that night.

After supper, he and Antonia spread their blankets underneath the wagon and turned in. Fargo knew that the Ovaro would alert him if anyone came near. He turned his attention to Antonia, and the two of them made love again, taking it slow and gentle at first, exploring almost every inch of each other's bodies with fingers and lips and tongues before finally coming together in another explosive, passionate union.

When Fargo finally slept, with Antonia in his arms, it was a deep and dreamless slumber, and he awoke the next morning feeling refreshed and eager to hit the trail again.

They had a fire this time, so they could boil coffee and heat up some tortillas and beans, and after breakfast Fargo hitched up the mules. The stallion tossed his head and nickered in irritation. Fargo chuckled and patted the big black-and-white horse's shoulder.

"You're getting tired of just following the wagon, aren't you, old boy?" he asked. He turned to Antonia, who was putting out the fire with handfuls of sand, and went on, "You reckon you could handle the team for a while this morning?"

"Of course, Skye," she replied. "What are you going to do?"

He got his saddle and saddle blanket from the back

of the wagon and started putting them on the Ovaro. "Thought I'd ride ahead a little and give my horse some exercise."

"Go ahead. Just don't go too far."

"I won't," he promised. "I'll stay in sight."

When they were back on the road, Fargo pulled ahead, letting the stallion stretch his legs. After galloping for a couple of hundred yards, though, Fargo pulled in the reins and brought the horse back to a walk. He looked over his shoulder and saw the wagon rolling along. Clearly, Antonia was having no trouble driving it.

The terrain flattened out even more as they continued south, although the brush country farther up the Nueces could hardly be considered mountainous, or even hilly. But this coastal plain was absolutely flat, and covered with scrubby growth that was only occasionally relieved by a small clump of trees. The landscape bore a striking resemblance to that of West Texas. The main difference was in the air. West Texas was dry, while here along the coast a thick layer of oppressive dampness lay over everything. Just riding down the road was enough to make a man break out in a sweat.

In late morning, when Fargo judged the stallion had had enough exercise, he trotted back to the wagon and tied the horse behind the vehicle again. Then he took the reins from Antonia and they pushed on.

The Nueces began to broaden as it neared the gulf. By midafternoon there was a wide stretch of blue water off to the left of the trail. Fargo saw a thin haze of smoke up ahead and knew it came from Corpus Christi. By late afternoon they reached the coastal settlement itself, which lay atop a shallow bluff that dropped down to the actual waterfront. Beyond the town, the vast blue-green Gulf of Mexico stretched as far as the eye could see.

Fargo was pretty much a landlubber at heart, but like most folks, the immensity of the ocean had a soothing effect on his soul. He drew back on the reins, brought the wagon to a halt, and gazed out over the gulf with its gentle, endless tides. "Mighty pretty," he murmured.

"Yes, it is," Antonia agreed. "I have heard my mother speak with great longing of the time she spent in Veracruz as a young woman, when my grandfather was the Spanish consul there. The gulf is beautiful there, too."

Fargo looked over at her. "I thought your mother and father met in Mexico City."

"It is true, they did. But that was later, after my mother lived for a time in Veracruz."

Fargo nodded. He hadn't been to Veracruz, far south on the Mexican coast, and knew it only as the site of some savage fighting during the war with Mexico a dozen years earlier. But he supposed the place had its own appeal to those who lived there.

They hadn't come this far just to sit and look at the gulf. He flapped the reins and got the mules moving again, following the road down the bluff to the waterfront, where the docks and warehouses and shipping offices were located. When they reached the street that paralleled the water, he asked a passerby where Lucas Peabody's warehouse was located.

"Go on down the street two blocks, and it'll be on your right," the man said.

Fargo nodded. "Much obliged."

A few minutes later he brought the wagon to a halt in front of a warehouse with a sign that read PEABODY IMPORTING AND EXPORTING. This was a rough neighborhood, with a lot of sailors and dockworkers on the street, so Fargo said to Antonia, "You'd better come inside with me."

She patted the rifle that lay on the seat beside her. "I do not think that anyone will bother me, Skye. If they do, they may regret it."

Fargo supposed she had proved she could take care of herself. He said, "All right," and jumped down from the seat. He went into the warehouse through the office door, talked to a clerk, and emerged a couple of minutes later with Lucas Peabody himself, a middle-aged man with a lined face, iron gray hair, and bushy side-whiskers.

"You say this is the shipment Rooster Jones was supposed to deliver to me?" he asked Fargo as he looked over the load of cotton.

"That's right," Fargo said, "minus one bale that was lost along the way. This is Rooster's wagon."

"What happened to that old pelican? How come he didn't bring this load in himself?"

Fargo explained, "He's laid up for a little while with a gunshot wound. Nothing serious, but he wasn't in good enough shape to make the rest of the trip down here."

"Who'd want to shoot a harmless old coot like Rooster?" Peabody asked with a frown.

"One of Johnny Lobo's men," Fargo said.

Peabody's eyes widened. "Lobo!"

"You've heard of him?"

"Everybody in this part of the country's heard of Johnny Lobo. He's held up the stage that runs between here and Victoria several times. He and his bunch haven't raided here in town yet, but folks are afraid that someday they might come riding in like a pack of wild Comanches and lay waste to the place."

Fargo shook his head. "I don't think Lobo's gang

is *that* big. There are enough of them to raise quite a bit of hell in the brasada, though."

"That's for sure." Peabody glanced up at Antonia, who was still on the wagon seat. "Excuse me, ma'am, but don't I know you?"

"This is Señorita Antonia Barrientos," Fargo said.

"Eduardo Barrientos' daughter?" Peabody sounded a little surprised.

"That is right, señor," Antonia said. "Are you acquainted with my father?"

Peabody nodded. "Yes, ma'am, I am. I met him a few years ago when he came through here on his way north to do some mustanging. He had his family with him then. I reckon that's where I saw you before."

"Yes, we stopped here in Corpus Christi, and I have been back several times since, when we came for supplies."

"Is Eduardo still chasing those mesteños?"

Antonia smiled. "Of course. He is working with a herd of them now, getting them ready to take to San Antonio. That is, if Johnny Lobo leaves them alone."

Peabody's face grew more solemn. "Yeah, the likes of Lobo might set his sights on a herd of mustangs."

Fargo put in, "We'll be heading back to the Barrientos' camp tomorrow. Rooster's there recuperating, and I plan to stay around until Señor Barrientos gets those mustangs sold."

"Well, give him my best," Peabody said. "If you want to leave the wagon here, my men will unload it and have it ready for you to take back tomorrow. I'll have the money for you then, too."

"That'll be fine," Fargo said with a nod. "In the meantime, where can we find a good hotel?"

With a calloused thumb, Peabody pointed toward the top of the bluff overlooking the waterfront. "The Nueces House on Upper Broadway is your best bet.

Rooms are clean, but they won't set you back an arm and a leg."

"Much obliged," Fargo said as he untied the Ovaro and Antonia's horse from the back of the wagon.

"Good to see you again, Señorita Barrientos. Give my best to your father."

"I will," Antonia said. She mounted up, as did Fargo, and they rode away from the warehouse and back toward the top of the bluff.

The Nueces House was easy to find, and it lived up to Peabody's recommendation. Fargo and Antonia took a couple of rooms for appearance's sake, although Fargo suspected they would be spending the night together again. Once they got back to the camp, of course, Fargo intended to treat Antonia with the utmost respect, not wishing to offend Señor and Señora Barrientos. For now, though, she was a fully grown young woman with healthy, lusty appetites, and they both intended to satisfy those appetites as frequently as possible.

Pleading weariness, Antonia said that she wanted to lie down for a while before they ate supper. Fargo agreed and took advantage of the opportunity to wash off some of the trail dust and change into a clean pair of buckskins. Early evening was coming on as he went across the hall and knocked softly on the door of Antonia's room.

When she opened it, his eyebrows went up in surprise. He had never seen her dressed in anything except denim trousers and a man's shirt, ready to ride or fight—until now.

She wore a low-cut, dark blue gown with flowing skirts. The bosom was trimmed with white lace. Her black hair was put up in an elaborate arrangement of curls, and somewhere she had found a bright red flower with which to adorn it. Clearly she hadn't spent all the time resting after all. Fargo thought she was breathtakingly lovely and said as much.

"*Gracias*, Skye," she said with a smile. "I wanted to look special for you, since this will be our only night in town."

"Well, you succeeded," Fargo told her. "I don't reckon there's a prettier woman in Corpus Christi tonight."

He took her arm and led her downstairs to the Nueces House's dining room. As they walked in, the male guests all looked at Antonia with admiration, and a few of them even sighed, probably in regret for their lost youth.

Dinner was good, if simple, and afterward Fargo and Antonia strolled along the bluff and looked out over the gulf as the last crimson vestiges of the day faded along the horizon behind them. The breeze off the water was soft and warm and made the evening that much more pleasant, although with Antonia's company it didn't really matter all that much what the weather was like.

When they returned to the hotel they went to Antonia's room, where Fargo paused at the door, letting her decide what would happen next. Her hand tightened on his and drew him into the room.

He lit the lamp but left it turned low. The gulf breeze stirred the curtains over the single window as Antonia began to get undressed. Fargo watched as she took off the blue gown, followed by her undergarments, until she stood nude before him, the lamplight glowing on her golden skin. As he stepped forward to take her in his arms, Fargo halfway expected something to happen—a knock on the door, a bullet through the window . . . something to ruin this moment. Trouble like that seemed to crop up all too often in his life.

But not this time. He drew Antonia into his embrace, brought his mouth down on hers, and caressed her nude, eager body. Her hands tugged at his buckskins, wanting them off so that there would be nothing between them, nothing to keep them apart.

A few minutes later, Fargo blew out the lamp. The gulf breeze continued to blow, not falling still until far into the night.

6

After a passionate but peaceful night, Fargo and Antonia had breakfast the next morning in the Nueces House's dining room and then rode down to the waterfront to pick up Rooster's wagon at Lucas Peabody's place of business. Antonia was back in trousers, a man's shirt, and boots and a hat this morning. Fargo liked her just fine that way, but he also knew it would be a long time before he forgot how she had looked at dinner the night before.

Peabody gave Fargo a bank draft for the cotton, which he would pass along to Rooster, who would deliver it in turn to the planters who had grown the cotton in the first place. Then, after shaking hands with Peabody, Fargo and Antonia climbed onto the wagon and headed north again. Their stay in Corpus Christi had been a short one, but Fargo would remember it fondly.

Without the load of cotton bales weighing down the wagon, the mule team was able to travel at a faster pace. Fargo pushed the mules a little, finding that he was anxious to get back to the mustang camp. A lot could have happened in the time that he and Antonia had been gone. With any luck, he thought, they would be able to reach the camp in a couple of days, with only one night spent on the trail.

That night, as he and Antonia lay naked on the blankets spread underneath the wagon, she swung a leg over his hips and straddled him. Reaching behind her, she grasped his erect member and guided it into her as she settled back and down onto him. Fargo's stiff shaft slid deeply into her. She closed her eyes and sighed in pleasure as she started to sit up straight.

With a little thud, the top of her head hit the underside of the wagon bed. She said, "Ouch!" and then giggled.

Fargo chuckled and said, "Be careful. Wouldn't want to knock yourself out."

"What do you care?" she teased. "You are a man. If I were unconscious, you would just go ahead and finish what you were doing anyway."

Fargo cupped her breasts and stroked her hardening nipples with his thumbs. "Yeah, well, it's a lot more enjoyable for both of us if you're awake."

Antonia's hips began to pump. She leaned forward and kissed him as he continued to caress her breasts. "Yes," she whispered, "a lot more enjoyable indeed."

Fargo met her thrusts with his own, and the pace of their coupling gradually increased until Antonia was riding him as if she were astride a galloping horse. Fargo moved his hands from her breasts to her bobbing hips to steady her. After several minutes of mounting passion, she drove down at him and he rose to meet her, and their culmination swept over them at the same time, leaving both of them limp and drained and breathless.

"Oh, Skye," Antonia said quietly when she had recovered somewhat and lay cuddled on his broad chest. "Tonight will be our last night together like this. When we return to the camp, we will not be able to do these things."

"I know," Fargo said. "It'll be rough, but I wouldn't want to upset your folks."

Antonia made a small, somehow ladylike snorting noise. "It is my sisters who would be the most upset if they knew what was between us. Elena and Ramona would want you for themselves."

"Ramona's just a kid."

"She is eighteen, Skye. I was married when I was eighteen. And I notice that you said nothing about Elena."

"Elena's a . . . mighty nice young woman," Fargo said carefully.

"She is a young woman who would like nothing more than to be exactly where I am right now, with you inside her as you are inside me."

Fargo's softening member gave a little jump at that thought.

"Oh, ho!" Antonia said. "So you want her, too, do you?"

"I never said that."

"Your body betrays you, Skye." Her lips brushed across his. "But do not worry, I am not angry. My sisters may want you, but I am the one who has you, at least for now. The night is long, eh?"

"Yes," Fargo agreed. "The night is long."

They didn't talk much until the next morning, but as they were headed up the road, Antonia said, "Thank you, Skye. It has been a long time since I have known the touch of a man."

"Always happy to oblige a beautiful woman."

She laughed but then grew serious. "No, I mean it. I mourned my husband for a long time, and I felt that I would never want any man again. You have proven to me that I must look forward again, not back."

"Well, if I helped, I'm glad," he said. "You mean a lot to me, too, Antonia."

She leaned her head against his shoulder and sighed. "Do you ever wish the world was different?"

He thought about the losses he had suffered in his life and said, "Of course. I reckon everybody does. But I've learned to deal with it as it is, to appreciate the good things and not let the bad things get me down. If you can't do that, you're liable to go loco."

"Yes. For a while, I believe that's what I was . . . loco. But no more."

Fargo smiled faintly and flapped the reins, clucking to the mules. Antonia had figured out that sooner or later he would be riding on, as he always did. She would be wasting her time thinking about any future they might have together, because Fargo never stayed in one place for long. From the sound of her words, she could accept that, and he was glad. He never wanted his fiddle-footed ways to cause anybody any pain . . . but he was too old to change now.

They passed through Dinero at midday, stopping there for a meal and a short visit with the Hagens, who were staying with Alex Wilson and his family until the hotel and saloon could be rebuilt. Quite a bit of work had been done since Fargo and Antonia had been there. The debris was all cleared away, and part of the framework of the new building was up.

"Seen any signs of Lobo and his men?" Fargo asked as he talked to Hagen and Wilson.

"My boy Thad was up on a ladder yesterday, working on the frame for Jack's new place," Wilson said. "He thought he saw a rider out in the brush, acting like he was keeping an eye on the settlement. Might have been Hector Rios, Thad said, but he wasn't sure."

Fargo nodded. "Could have been. Anybody who wasn't up to no good would have been on the road. Maybe Rios was waiting for me to come back."

"You think Johnny Lobo will want to take revenge on the whole town?" Hagen asked.

"You never know how an outlaw's mind is going to work. Chances are, though, Lobo knows that I'm responsible for the deaths of Sanderson and DeWalt. If he wants to settle that score, he'll have to settle it with me."

That seemed to ease the minds of the townspeople a little, but Fargo knew they would still worry as long as Lobo and his gang were on the loose.

As he and Antonia left Dinero behind and started north again, she said, "This business with Johnny Lobo is not over yet, is it, Skye?"

"My gut tells me it's not," he replied after mulling the question over for a moment. "Lobo didn't get to be the leader of a band of outlaws by letting defeats go unavenged. I got away from him when he jumped me in the chaparral, then I helped run him off when he tried to steal your father's herd. Then there was the business with Sanderson and DeWalt." Fargo shook his head. "No, I reckon we haven't seen the last of Johnny Lobo."

There weren't many landmarks in a countryside distinguished by seemingly endless stretches of thorny brush, but by late afternoon Fargo began to get the sense that they were approaching the location of the mustang camp. When he said something about it to Antonia, she confirmed his hunch.

"The camp is no more than a mile or two from here," she said. "We should reach it soon."

It wasn't more than a couple of minutes later when Fargo's eyes narrowed as he looked ahead. "I see some smoke up there," he said.

"Probably from the campfire," Antonia replied.

Fargo shook his head. "There's too much of it for that. See?"

He leveled an arm and pointed, and beside him on the seat, Antonia stiffened. "You're right," she said, worry in her voice. "That is about where the camp should be, too. Do you think something's wrong, Skye?"

"We're about to find out," Fargo said. He slapped the reins hard against the backs of the mules and shouted at them. The animals broke into a run. The wagon bounced in the ruts of the trail as it picked up speed.

Antonia levered a round into the chamber of her rifle as they approached the campsite. The column of smoke climbing into the sky was thicker and darker now, and Fargo knew it didn't come from any campfire. They came to the place where the river had to be forded and the wagon wheels rattled across the rocky streambed.

Fargo swung the mules around a clump of brush and the camp came into sight, lying against the low bluff about a quarter of a mile away. He saw flames now at the base of the smoke, and knew that the brush fence that enclosed the mustangs was on fire. When the chaparral was hacked loose from its roots and piled up, it remained as thorny as ever, providing a near-impenetrable barrier, but after it dried out it burned easily.

Fargo knew there was no reason Eduardo Barrientos would have purposely set his corral on fire. The blaze had to mean there had been some real trouble here. The absence of gunshots in the hot afternoon air made Fargo think that trouble was over, though—at least temporarily.

"Madre de Dios!" Antonia exclaimed as they came closer and saw that the gate was down. Not just open, but knocked down, wrecked. A slender figure ran out of the corral, waving urgently. Antonia said, "That's Ramona!"

Fargo recognized the youngest of the Barrientos sisters, too. Ramona had a rifle in her hands and fired it twice into the air, as if to hurry the wagon along, but the mules were already running as hard as they could. Fargo didn't slow them until they reached the camp. Antonia leaped down from the wagon even before it completely came to a skidding, shuddering halt. The dust cloud that had been kicked up by the mules drifted over the camp and mingled with the smoke from the burning brush.

Antonia ran over to Ramona and caught hold of her shoulders. Fargo was close behind her and saw how upset and frightened Ramona was. There were also bloodstains on her shirt, but she didn't act like she was wounded. That meant the blood probably belonged to someone else.

"Ramona!" Antonia cried. "What happened? Are you all right?"

"It . . . it was Johnny Lobo!" Ramona gasped. "He and his men, they came out of nowhere!" Tears ran down her cheeks. "I was watching, but I never saw them until they were on us—"

"Papa! Mama!" Antonia shook her younger sister. "Where are they? Where is Elena?"

"Gone!" Ramona wailed. "Mama and Elena are gone! Lobo took them, along with the mustangs! And Papa—" She shuddered. "They shot Papa!"

So that blood on her shirt had probably come from Eduardo Barrientos, Fargo thought as he looked past

Ramona into the corral. It was empty now, all the wild horses gone, and the only signs of life were over by the bluff, where Barrientos sat with his back propped against a rock and old Rooster Jones knelt beside him.

Fargo left Antonia trying to comfort the weeping Ramona and strode over to Rooster and Barrientos. Rooster appeared to be all right, other than the stiffness left over from the wound he had suffered several days earlier. Barrientos' shirt was off and had been torn into strips, which were now bound around his torso in a couple of places. A similar makeshift bandage, bloodstained like the others, was wrapped around his forehead. He was unconscious. His chest rose and fell as he breathed raggedly.

"I'm mighty glad to see you, Fargo," Rooster said. "Wish you'd been here about an hour ago, when them skalleyhooters hit us. Might've been a different story if you had been."

"Sorry, Rooster. We got back as quickly as we could."

Rooster waved a gnarled hand. "I know, son, I know. I ain't blamin' you. It was that no-good Johnny Lobo who was responsible for this."

"Tell me what happened," Fargo said.

"They snuck up on us like a bunch o' damned Comanch', that's what happened. Some of 'em crawled up and set fire to the brush while the others opened up on us. The flames and the smoke spooked those mustangs so bad they busted down the gate and damn near trampled us while we was tryin' to fight back. Then Lobo his own self and a couple other men swooped in on horseback and grabbed up Señora Barrientos and Elena. Eduardo tried to stop 'em and like to got hisself shot to pieces. Me an' Ramona grabbed him and got him inside the fence, then we put up as much of a fight as we could. Lobo's bunch wasn't really interested by then, though. They had the mustangs and they had Señora Barrientos and Elena, so they pulled back and took off, headed north.''

Fargo looked down at the unconscious Barrientos. "You patched him up?"

"Yeah, best I could with Ramona's help. I ain't no sawbones, though. Don't know if he'll make it or not. He was shot a couple times through the body and got a nasty bullet crease on his head. If them two slugs didn't hit anything too vital in his innards, he might pull through.''

Fargo nodded. Barrientos was pale, but his breathing seemed fairly regular. "The bullets went all the way through? He's not still carrying any lead in him?"

"That's right," Rooster said.

"All right." Fargo's tone was decisive as he went on, "We'll put some blankets in the back of the wagon to make a pallet and load him in there. Antonia and Ramona can take him down to Dinero. There's no doctor there, but I'd be willing to bet that Father Pascual at the mission has done his share of caring for injured and wounded men.''

"Yeah, I know that ol' padre," Rooster agreed. "He'll do a good job o' taking care of Eduardo. What's that leave you and me doin'?"

"We're going to go after Lobo and get those women and the mustangs back from him," Fargo said.

"Just the two of us against Lobo and his whole gang o' murderin' cutthroats?"

"That's all we've got," Fargo said. "Just the two of us."

A grin suddenly spread across Rooster's weathered face. He spat on the ground and said, "That bastard Lobo ain't got no idea what sort o' trouble he's in for now.''

Antonia argued with the decision, which came as no surprise to Fargo.

"We should let Señor Rooster go with Ramona to take my father to Dinero," she said. "I will come with you, Skye."

Fargo shook his head. "Not a good idea."

"*Dios mio!* Señor Rooster is an old man, and injured as well! You know I can shoot and fight, Skye!"

"I know it, which is why you need to go with Ramona and your father, to make sure they get to Dinero safely."

Rooster put in, "And I'm feelin' a heap more spry now, after restin' up for a few days."

"You do not fool me, either of you," Antonia said darkly. "You will not take me along because I am a woman."

"It's just better for you to go with your father and your sister," Fargo said. "You can handle that team without any trouble. You'll have to drive on into the night because Señor Barrientos needs to get there as soon as he can, without being jostled around too much. I know you're worried about your mother and Elena, but your father's life is in your hands, Antonia."

She sighed, as if giving in to his argument but not liking it a bit. "All right, Skye. But I don't see how you have any chance of getting Mama and Elena back from Lobo."

"Well, we can't outfight them, so we'll have to be sneaky about it. My figuring is that Lobo has a camp of his own somewhere, a hideout in the brasada where he and his gang go when they're not out raising hell. They'll probably head for that camp now. It's up to Rooster and me to find it, get in there somehow, and get the women out before Lobo knows what's going on."

"What about the mustangs?"

"Once your mother and Elena are safe, then we'll work on figuring out a way to get the horses back, too. But rescuing the prisoners comes first."

Antonia nodded. "Of course. Let's get the wagon ready for my father."

Once she had accepted the idea, she threw herself into the preparations and soon had a thick bed of blankets in the back of the wagon. Fargo, Antonia, and Ramona carefully picked up the still-unconscious Barrientos and transferred him into the vehicle. Ramona drew a blanket over him to keep him warm. He had lost enough blood that he might get chilled easily, even in this warm weather.

Antonia and Ramona climbed onto the wagon seat. Ramona had dried her tears and was more composed now. She held her rifle across her lap while Antonia took up the reins.

"Be careful, Skye," Antonia said as she looked down at Fargo.

"I intend to be," he said. "I don't think you'll run into any trouble, but you and Ramona keep a sharp eye out, anyway."

"Of course." A look passed between them, a look that spoke of the intimacies they had shared, mixed with the concern they felt for each other as they set out on their respective missions.

Then Antonia slapped the reins against the backs of the mules and got the team moving. Fargo and Rooster stood there for a moment, watching the wagon roll toward the Nueces River and the trail beyond that would take it to Dinero.

"Them gals are tough as whang leather," Rooster said. "They'll be all right."

Fargo nodded. "Come on. We'd better get on Lobo's trail."

Antonia had left her horse behind for Rooster to ride. The old-timer was taking Eduardo Barrientos' rifle with him, along with the cap-and-ball pistol he normally carried. He and Fargo salvaged what supplies they could from the wreckage of the camp. Then they mounted up, circled the bluff, and headed north.

According to Rooster, the attack on the camp had taken place about an hour earlier. A little more than that, now, since it had taken some time to make the preparations for their departure. As they rode along, Fargo asked, "Were the outlaws trying to round up those mustangs, or did they just let them run loose?"

"Lobo had enough men so they were able to turn the stampede and get them mesteños movin' the way they wanted 'em to go. Eduardo'd already done rubbed a bunch o' the raw off 'em, so they weren't near as wild as they started out. I reckon Lobo will be able to keep 'em herded and movin' along without too much trouble."

"I was hoping maybe the mustangs would slow them down, and they still will to a certain extent. But the gang's got a good lead on us."

"One thing, though," Rooster said as he pointed to the ground ahead of them, where the hoofprints of many horses were visible. "Drivin' that many critters leaves sign even a bleary-eyed ol' pelican like me can follow, and I ain't even a Trailsman!"

Despite the grim circumstances, Fargo had to smile a little. Rooster had a point.

Going anywhere in the brasada in a straight line was just about impossible. Whenever a stretch of chaparral popped up, travelers had no choice but to go around it or find a path through it. The same thing was true of the herd of mustangs being driven by Lobo's men. They continued moving in a generally northerly direction, but there were plenty of detours to the east and west. A man could get lost in this jungle of thorns and perhaps never find his way out.

In the late afternoon, Fargo heard a grunting sound somewhere up ahead. Rooster heard it, too, and said, "Uh-oh."

"What is it?" Fargo asked as they both reined in.

"Javelinas."

Fargo was expecting that answer. He had encountered the beasts before and thought he recognized their distinctive grunts.

They were fierce wild hogs with bony backs, bristly hides, and sharp tusks. Usually on the scrawny, smallish side, they ran in packs, and any man unlucky enough to be set upon by them would likely be ripped to shreds in minutes by those tusks. Occasionally a javelina grew larger than usual and became a real monster, capable of taking down a cow or horse by itself. They were just about the only animals that could make their way fairly easily through the chaparral. Their thick hides could withstand the mesquite thorns.

Fargo drew his Henry from the saddle sheath as the grunting grew louder. He didn't want to take on a whole pack of javelinas, even with the fifteen-shot repeater. They were proddy beasts to start with, easily angered and maniacal in their fury once they were riled up. They would tear at the legs of a horse until it collapsed, dumping its rider in their midst. When a man went down in a pack of javelinas, it was all over for him.

"There they are," Rooster said quietly.

Fargo saw the animals come boiling out of the brush about a hundred yards away. They were going the other direction, but that didn't mean much. Javelinas didn't see too well, but they had a keen sense of smell and the wind was behind Fargo and Rooster and their horses. Fargo tensed as he saw the pack stop. The ugly grunting fell silent. The animals lifted their muzzles and sniffed, as if trying to decide whether to swing around and swarm over the two riders.

Then they started grunting again and took off toward the east, evidently deciding they were more interested in something over there. Rooster heaved a sigh of relief as the javelinas disappeared back into the chaparral and the sound of their grunting diminished.

"I hate them damn varmints," the old-timer said with considerable feeling.

"I'm not too fond of them myself," Fargo said. He slid the rifle back into the saddle boot. "Let's go before they decide to come back."

The two men pushed on, still following the trail of the stolen mustangs. The sun was low on the western horizon by now, and Fargo realized they weren't going to catch up to Lobo's bunch before nightfall. They couldn't risk trying to follow the trail after dark. If they lost it, they might not ever find it again in this brushy wasteland. That meant they would have to stop and wait for morning.

Rooster shared the same worry. The old man said, "You reckon Lobo will push on through the night? He prob'ly knows where he's goin', so he don't have to worry about followin' a trail."

"He might," Fargo admitted. "That means we'll be even farther behind by tomorrow morning."

"I hope them damn owlhoots are keepin' their hands off them gals. It sure gnaws at my innards, worryin' about what might be happenin' to 'em."

"Mine, too," Fargo said, "but dwelling on it isn't going to do us any good. All we can do is stay on their trail. We'll catch up to them sooner or later."

"Yeah . . . and then all we got to do is snatch them two women away from twenty-five or thirty o' the most bloodthirsty killers in all o' Texas."

Fargo smiled. "You knew the job was dangerous when you took it."

Rooster just snorted.

The sun continued its plummet, and a few minutes later it had disappeared below the horizon. Dusky shadows gathered quickly. A few stars began to wink into existence in the arching, deep blue sky overhead where it shaded into purple and then black. Fargo kept the stallion moving. He wanted to follow the trail as long as he possibly could.

A few minutes later, though, as the light breeze shifted around to the north, he reined in sharply and motioned for Rooster to do the same. He sat stiffly in the saddle.

"What is it?" Rooster asked, instinctively whispering.

"Smell that?" Fargo whispered back.

Rooster sniffed a couple of times and then looked over at Fargo, his eyes widening in the dimness. "That's wood smoke," he said, "and somethin' else. . . . Roastin' meat? But that likely means . . ."

"That's right," Fargo said. "I reckon we've found them."

7

They dismounted and led their horses forward, knowing that it was important to be quiet now. Sound always seemed to travel better at night, and darkness was swiftly falling over the brush country.

They came to a wall of brush and had to stop. The chaparral was thick and forbidding.

"Got to be a way through it," Rooster whispered. "That smoke's comin' from the other side somewheres. But how'll we find it?"

Fargo looked along the edge of the chaparral. It seemed to be a solid dark line in the gathering gloom, and he couldn't see the end of it in either direction. He knew that the thicket might stretch for miles.

"You go east and I'll go west," he told Rooster. "Can you howl like a coyote?"

Rooster's teeth flashed in a grin. "The ol' Comanche trick, eh? Yeah, I can do that."

"Then sing out if you find a trail. I'll do the same."

"You don't reckon it'll make them owlhoots suspicion somethin'?"

"Not if we're careful," Fargo said. "Good luck."

"We're liable to need it," Rooster said.

The two men parted. Fargo walked east along the brush wall. As the sky grew darker and the last vestiges of daylight faded away, he had to put out a hand from time to time to make sure how big the gaps in the brush were. The thorns pricked his fingers. As the minutes passed, he didn't find any openings large enough for even a single man on horseback to pass through.

He lifted his head suddenly as he heard a high-pitched, yipping cry from east of his position. It lasted only a moment, but it was enough to make Fargo wheel around and lead the Ovaro in that direction. Rooster had done a good job imitating a coyote. He had sounded just like the real thing. If any of the outlaws had heard it, Fargo didn't think they would suspect anything.

A few minutes later, a couple of dark shapes loomed out of the shadows. Fargo recognized them as Rooster and the horse he was leading. "You found a trail?" Fargo whispered.

"Right over here." Rooster gestured behind him.

Fargo didn't see it at first. The opening seemed to blend in with the rest of the chaparral. But then his keen eyes picked it out, a gap in the brush barely six feet wide.

"I don't know how they got them mustangs through there," Rooster went on.

"One at a time, just like they had to ride through it themselves." The trail wasn't large enough for more than one man on horseback. Fargo sniffed the air. "It probably took a while for them to get the herd through, so the mustangs milled around here quite a bit. You can still smell the dust in the air."

"Yeah, I reckon that's right. What're we gonna do?"

"We'd better leave the horses here and go ahead on foot," Fargo decided. "We can move more quietly that way."

"Don't much like bein' without a mount," Rooster said dubiously.

"Neither do I, but we don't want to announce that we're coming, either."

Rooster couldn't argue with that, so they tied the two horses to a small tree a few feet away from the edge of the chaparral. Then they took their rifles and started into the brush.

Fargo didn't expect the trail to run straight, but it twisted around even more than usual, starting almost as soon as they were inside the thicket. Even in broad daylight it would be difficult to see the trail unless a person was almost right on top of it. You could ride by fifty yards away and never even notice the opening. That explained why Lobo and his men used it. Outlaws were always on the lookout for good hiding places. It was in their nature to be furtive.

The smell of wood smoke and roasting meat grew stronger. They were getting close to the gang's camp. Fargo heard a shrill whinny that probably came from one of the mustangs. It seemed like he and Rooster had walked for at least a mile, but he knew that probably they had penetrated only a few hundred yards into the chaparral. The twists and turns of the trail just made it seem longer.

Suddenly, he caught a glimpse of a red glow up ahead and stopped, putting out a hand to bring Rooster to a halt as well. Fargo studied the light. It was indirect, a reflection of flames rather than the flames themselves. Slowly and carefully, he paced forward again.

He went to a knee and drew Rooster down beside him as they reached yet another bend in the trail. This one was different, though. Around it the brush fell away on either side of the trail, opening into a huge clearing ringed all around by the thorny barrier. The clearing was at least half a mile wide, and in the middle was a small lake, the sort known in this part of the country as a resaca. Fed by deep springs, no creek led into or out of it. All the water was contained inside the clearing.

Several shacks built of mesquite poles sat near the lake. One building was larger and sturdier, constructed of rough planks that must have been brought in from outside somehow. It had a thatched roof and a porch across the front of it. Fargo wondered if that was where Johnny Lobo lived. As the leader of the gang, he probably had the best accommodations. A large bonfire blazed between the big house and the shacks, throwing its light across nearly the entire clearing.

A pole corral had been built for the outlaws' horses. Movement on the far side of the lake caught Fargo's eye, and he looked over to see the herd of mustangs, moving around some but held in place by several men on horseback. The herders' task was made easier by the wall of brush against which the mustangs were backed up.

"Lord, they got 'em a reg'lar settlement here, almost," Rooster breathed.

"I knew they had to have a good hideout somewhere," Fargo said. "Lobo wouldn't be able to hold together a band of that size without having someplace for them to go between jobs."

"You know, I think I heard o' this here lake. It ain't a reg'lar resaca. It's deeper than usual, and it's supposed to be haunted."

Fargo looked over at the old-timer. "Haunted?"

"Yeah. When the ol' Spaniards first come to these parts, they took the Injuns who wouldn't cooperate and threw 'em in the lake. Drownded a whole bunch that way. I've heard it said the spirits o' them dead Injuns still haunt this lake."

Fargo had heard plenty of ghost stories in his time; the frontier was rife with them. Sometimes their origins had some basis in fact. He didn't doubt for a second that the Spanish conquerors might have disposed of some troublesome Indians in this lake. He didn't much believe in the spirit part of the story, though.

"I'm more worried about live outlaws," he whispered to Rooster.

"Yeah, me too. Looks like they're all here."

The members of the gang were gathered around the fire, where haunches from a butchered steer were roasting at the edge of the leaping flames. Bottles and jugs were being passed back and forth. The men had to be celebrating the theft of the mustang herd, which would fetch a good price.

Fargo thought he saw Hector Rios, who was supposedly Johnny Lobo's second in command, but he didn't see Lobo himself. The bandit chieftain was big enough that he would be hard to miss. Fargo didn't see Juliana or Elena, either, and he had to wonder if the two women were in the house along with Lobo. That thought made an icy finger run down his spine.

"Now what?" Rooster asked.

The wheels of Fargo's brain were turning over rapidly as he began to formulate a plan. "We wait a while," he said. "The way those men are drinking, some of them will be passed out in another hour or so."

Rooster frowned. "Lots o' things can happen in an hour, most of 'em bad."

Fargo knew he was worried about Juliana and Elena, and he shared the old-timer's concern. But there was nothing else they could do.

"I think the women must be inside the house with Lobo, and with the way that fire's burning so brightly, there's no way we could reach the place without being spotted. But if we let it burn down some, and let them guzzle that who-hit-John for a while, our chances of getting in without being seen will be a lot better."

"Yeah, I reckon that's right," Rooster grumbled. "Don't have to like it, though."

"No," Fargo agreed, "we don't have to like it."

As they settled down to wait, Fargo continued to study the situation. He thought that if they were patient, they could get into the house. Getting out might be a different story. Lobo wouldn't let his captives go without a fight, and any commotion from the house might alarm the whole camp.

What they needed was something else to alarm it, he realized. Something to cause so much confusion and panic that the outlaws wouldn't be worried about their prisoners getting away.

Fargo's gaze kept coming back to those mustangs on the other side of the lake. . . .

The celebration around the fire continued, with the laughter coming from the outlaws growing louder and more raucous as they drank more and more. They used their knives to cut chunks off the sizzling beef haunches, and slumped on the ground to gnaw at the meat. As Fargo watched, one of the men tipped his head far back to drink from a jug, and he just kept going. The jug fell from his hand unnoticed as he sprawled in a drunken stupor.

That was what Fargo wanted to see, and as the minutes dragged by, it began to happen more and more often. Not all the men passed out, of course, but before too much longer, at least half of the two dozen men around the fire were asleep.

Fargo put a hand on Rooster's shoulder and said into the old-timer's ear, "Here's what you're going to do. Work your way around the edge of the clearing until you're over there close to those mustangs. When you get there, start shooting and yelling."

"Say, I get the idea! You want me to stampede those critters, just like Lobo stampeded 'em back at the Barrientos' camp."

"That's right," Fargo said. "There's nowhere for them to go except around the lake and right into that bunch of outlaws."

"The herders'll try to stop 'em. Reckon when I go to shootin', I'd better try to ventilate them buzzards."

"That's up to you, Rooster."

The old man grunted. "Don't think I'll lose any sleep over pluggin' those varmints. If they're ridin' with Lobo, they got plenty o' innocent blood on their hands, by God!"

Fargo nodded and said, "Just stay as close as you can to the chaparral, where the light from the fire won't be as likely to reach you."

"All right, son, but it's gonna take me a while to get around there."

"That's fine. I'll be busy in the meantime. I want to get into that house and find the women. With any luck, I'll be ready to bring them out about the same time you stampede the mustangs. We'll meet outside the chaparral, where we left the horses."

Rooster nodded and put out a gnarled, calloused hand. "Good luck to you, Fargo."

Fargo shook with him. "Good luck to you, too, Rooster."

In a crouch, Rooster moved off to the right, making his way around the edge of the clearing. He was so close to the brush that the thorns caught at his clothes from time to time. Fargo watched him for a few moments until he was no longer able to see the old-timer. He knew that if he couldn't see Rooster, then neither could the outlaws over by the fire. The blaze had died down somewhat from its previous height, and the reddish-yellow glare didn't reach as far anymore.

But it still illuminated the area around the shacks and the house, and that was where Fargo needed to go. Following in Rooster's footsteps, he started around the edge of the clearing. He planned to use the house itself to cover his approach, putting the structure between himself, the shacks, and the bonfire.

The chaparral wasn't made up entirely of mesquite. There was a lot of undergrowth as well, such as prickly pear and catclaw, and those plants were just as thorny and troublesome. More than once, a stickery branch seemed to leap out and grab at Fargo, even though he knew that wasn't really the case. By the time he was in position, he was covered with scratches just from being near the stuff.

But he ignored the stinging pain and concentrated on the task at hand. There was a lighted window in the end of the house that faced toward him, although a shade had been lowered over it. Still, if anyone happened to look out that window, they might see him. To minimize the chances of that, he got down on his belly and began to crawl toward the house.

Part of the way there, he heard something slither through the grass near him and froze. Fat diamondback rattlesnakes were common in the brush country, and he figured he had disturbed one of them on its nightly rounds. He waited for the telltale buzz of rattles, but the ominous sound didn't come. Instead, as

Fargo listened intently, he heard the snake slithering farther away. He realized he had been holding his breath and blew it out in a quiet sigh of relief.

Then he continued crawling himself, heading toward the cabin and keeping his eyes fixed on the dim rectangle of light that marked the window.

Fargo could hear the men by the fire still talking and laughing, but they were a lot quieter now because so many of them were asleep. If he had been willing to wait, they might have all passed out sooner or later, except for a few guards. But that would have taken all night, and he couldn't leave the two women in the house for that long. They had already been in Lobo's hands for too long.

The window was only about ten yards away now. Fargo came up on his hands and knees, then surged to his feet and sprinted silently across that last bit of ground. He dropped into a crouch underneath the window and listened.

The house seemed to be silent at first, as if it were deserted, and he had a bad moment when he wondered if Lobo and the prisoners were even in there. But then he heard the low rumble of a man's voice, answered a second later by a woman's softer tones. He couldn't hear either one clearly enough to make out the words, or even to be sure that they belonged to Lobo and either Juliana or Elena, but his instincts told him that they did.

Fargo straightened and moved the window shade aside just enough to look into the room. To his surprise, he saw the foot of a four-poster bed. The outlaws must have had a chore getting *that* into this brush country stronghold. A thick rug lay on the floor beside the bed, and Fargo could also see part of a handsome dressing table where a small lamp burned. Obviously, Lobo liked his luxuries.

No one was in the bedroom, and the door opposite the window was closed. Fargo leaned his rifle against the outside wall, got a good hold on the windowsill, and pulled himself up and over, making as little noise as possible as he slid into the room. He crouched just inside the window for a moment, waiting to see if his entrance had been detected.

He heard voices again on the other side of the door, but they didn't sound alarmed. Fargo cat-footed across the room and leaned close to the door, turning his head so that his ear was close to the tiny gap around the door. He wanted to hear what was going on in the other room so he could figure out what to do next.

What he heard were heavy footsteps approaching the door. He drew back quickly so that he would be behind the door when it opened and pressed his back against the wall. He slipped the Colt out of its holster and waited. If Lobo stepped into the room, Fargo intended to knock him out.

The door opened, but it wasn't Johnny Lobo who came into the room. In the light that spilled from the other room, Fargo recognized the womanly figure and dark blond hair of Juliana Barrientos. She was followed closely, though, by the tall, burly Lobo. Anger flared inside Fargo. The bastard was bringing Juliana in here to rape her!

Fargo didn't know if there were any other men inside the house. He had heard only Lobo's voice, but that was no guarantee that none of the other outlaws were here. He couldn't afford to wait. Either Lobo or Juliana could turn around at any second and see him. Fargo wasn't confident that Juliana could conceal her surprise if it was she who spotted him.

So he struck while he had the chance, hard and fast.

The hand holding the Colt went up and then flashed down. With a dull thud, the barrel slammed into

Lobo's head. Fargo didn't particularly care whether he shattered the man's skull, so he didn't hold back. Lobo grunted as the blow fell, stumbled forward a step, went to his knees, and then pitched forward onto his face, hitting the floor like a falling tree.

Startled, Juliana turned and leaped back away from Lobo. She saw Fargo then and her eyes widened with shock. Her mouth opened. Fearing that she was so unnerved by the ordeal she had suffered so far that she might scream, Fargo lunged forward and clapped his free hand over her mouth.

"It's me, Señora Barrientos. Skye Fargo." He whispered the words into her ear. "I've come to get you and Elena out of here."

She stared at him for a long moment, her eyes so big they looked like they might come out of her head. But then, abruptly, she seemed to understand. She jerked her head in a nod.

Fargo took his hand away from her mouth and asked, "Where's Elena?" Rooster would be stampeding those mustangs any time now, and Fargo wanted to have the women ready to go when all hell broke loose.

"In . . . in the other room," Juliana gasped.

"Is she all right?"

"She is tied up, but she has not been hurt. I saw to that."

Probably bargained for better treatment for her daughter by promising Lobo she would do anything he wanted, Fargo thought. Leaving Juliana where she was, he turned swiftly to the door and stepped through it.

Elena sat in a chair on the other side of the room, her wrists tied together in front of her. She stood up quickly, looking just as surprised as her mother had, and exclaimed, "Señor Fargo!"

Fargo switched the Colt to his left hand and reached down with his right to draw the Arkansas toothpick. "Hold your arms out," he told Elena as he straightened with the big knife in his hand. One quick but careful stroke of the blade severed the rope bonds.

"You . . . you have come to save us?"

Fargo nodded. "Yes, we're getting out of here. Come on."

"But Lobo—"

"He won't be waking up for a while." Fargo sheathed the knife, switched the revolver back to his right hand, and grasped Elena's arm with his left hand.

"But my mother—"

"She's all right."

Fargo hustled Elena into the bedroom. Juliana still stood there, gazing down at Lobo's unconscious form with an unreadable expression on her face. After everything the outlaw had done, Fargo wouldn't have blamed Juliana if she had wanted to borrow his knife and cut the bastard's throat. Instead, Juliana just seemed sort of numb as Fargo prodded her and Elena toward the window.

"Any minute now, we'll have the distraction we need in order to reach the chaparral," he told them.

That is, if nothing had happened to Rooster. If the old-timer should happen to fail . . .

Suddenly, a rattle of gunfire erupted somewhere outside. Fargo heard the crack of a rifle, the dull boom of a cap-and-ball revolver, and several strident shouts. The racket was followed immediately by a growing rumble.

Hoofbeats. The mustangs were stampeding, just like Fargo and Rooster had planned.

"Out the window!" he said to Juliana and Elena. "Fast!"

Elena went first, throwing a leg over the sill and

practically leaping out into the night. Juliana was still moving slowly, so stunned by the unexpected turn of events that it was almost like she didn't want to escape. Fargo hustled her out the window and then dropped to the ground beside her. As he snatched up his rifle, he said, "Head for the chaparral! Follow me and I'll get you out of here!"

He had marked the location of the trail in his head, so he knew his instincts would lead him back there unerringly. More shots blasted in the darkness, the thundering hoofbeats grew louder, and somebody screamed, a shriek that was cut off abruptly, probably by the trampling hooves of the runaway mustangs.

Fargo wanted to get the women out of the way before the stampede reached this point. The clearing was circular, so the wild horses had no place to go except around the camp and the lake. Elena stayed right with him as he hurried toward the chaparral, but when he looked back, he saw that Juliana continued to lag. Fargo dropped back and reached for her arm. "Señora, you got to come on—" he began.

That was when a voice roared out, so loud it was audible even over the gunshots and the stampeding mustangs.

"Stop them! Over there! Stop them, damn your eyes!"

Fargo's head jerked around and he saw the huge figure of Johnny Lobo standing on the porch of the house, rubbing his head. The man's skull had to be as hard as cast iron for him to have recovered so quickly from the clout Fargo had given him.

Some of the outlaws had managed to get to their horses and were trying to bring the stampeding mustangs under control. Others were just trying to get out of the way before they got trampled. But a few turned and ran toward Fargo and the two women. Guns appeared in their hands and muzzle flame jabbed toward the fugitives. Fargo brought the Henry to his shoulder and fired three times, cranking off the shots as fast as he could work the rifle's lever. One man was driven backward by the slug that struck him, while another went spinning crazily off his feet. Seeing two of their number fall like that made the other bandits hesitate.

"Hold your fire!" Lobo bellowed as he came down from the porch and started toward Fargo, Elena, and Juliana in a shambling run. "No shooting! You might hit the women!"

That gave Fargo a little respite. If Juliana would come on, they still had a chance to reach the winding path through the chaparral. From there Fargo thought they might be able to elude the pursuit.

The mustangs were only about a hundred yards away now, some of them running wildly out of control while others were starting to slow down and mill around. The stampede wasn't over, though, and it still posed a danger to Fargo and his companions.

So did a couple of outlaws on horseback who spurred toward them. Fargo whipped the Henry up again and fired a couple of times. One of the men sagged in his saddle, but the other pounded on, bearing down on the Trailsman. Fargo had to leap aside to keep from being trampled.

He looked around for Elena and Juliana. Elena was still running toward the chaparral, but Juliana had veered off and seemed to be confused. The way she was heading, Lobo would intercept her before she reached safety. Fargo opened his mouth to call a warning to her, but before he could say anything a bullet whipped past his ear. Somebody had disregarded Lobo's order not to shoot.

Fargo didn't have to worry about disobeying that order. He twisted and saw that the shot had come from the man on horseback he had just avoided. The rifle in Fargo's hand blasted again just as flame spurted a second time from the outlaw's gun. The man pitched sideways out of the saddle, hit solidly by Fargo's shot.

Hoofbeats made him spin. He saw that he was between a rock and a hard place. One of the runaway mustangs was galloping toward him, and bearing down on him even closer was Johnny Lobo, his bearded face contorted by rage.

Lobo launched himself in a diving tackle that slammed into Fargo and knocked him off his feet. Both men went down, rolling out of the way of the stampeding mustang. More of the wild horses surged past them, legs flashing, hooves striking the ground only inches away from the struggling men. Fargo had dropped his rifle when Lobo crashed into him. He tried to reach for his Colt or the Arkansas toothpick, but Lobo got his arms around Fargo, pinning him in a bear hug. The man was amazingly strong and outweighed Fargo. It was only a matter of time until he crushed the breath and the life out of his opponent.

Desperately, Fargo brought his knee up into Lobo's groin. The man grunted in pain, and his grip loosened enough for Fargo to get his left arm loose. He chopped with the side of his hand at the center of Lobo's face, hoping to shatter the big man's nose and maybe even drive bone splinters up into his brain. Lobo ducked his head at the last second, though, so Fargo's blow landed on his forehead. It was painful, but not incapacitating.

Fargo tried again for Lobo's groin. Lobo howled this time and rolled over, his massive arms flinging Fargo away from him. Fargo hit the ground hard. The impact knocked the breath out of his lungs, and for a second all he could do was lie there and gasp for air.

That second was long enough for Lobo to rise up and draw a long-barreled revolver from his belt. He loomed over Fargo like a mountain and drew back the hammer. Fargo found himself staring upward into the barrel of the gun, with death only a hair-trigger pull away.

Then, suddenly, Juliana Barrientos was beside Lobo, but instead of striking at him she clutched his arm as if in supplication and cried, "Don't, John! Please! Please don't kill him!"

As Fargo looked up, a second ticked by in an eternity, and then Lobo carefully lowered the gun's hammer. He looked over at Juliana with a smile and said, "Whatever you want, m'love."

8

Fargo was too stunned by what he had just heard to do anything except lie there. Most of the stampeding mustangs had already galloped past. A couple of the outlaws ran up to Lobo, who pointed a hamlike hand at Fargo and growled, "Get him on his feet and take him in the house."

Strong hands reached down and hauled Fargo upright. His Colt and the Arkansas toothpick were plucked from their sheaths. Another of the men picked up the Henry rifle Fargo had dropped.

Juliana still clung to Lobo's arm. Fargo glanced around quickly but didn't see any sign of Elena. He hoped she had reached the chaparral and found the trail through it. Maybe she had gotten away and managed to rendezvous with Rooster.

It was becoming obvious to Fargo that he had been wrong about Juliana. He had thought she was just stunned and confused by everything that had happened, but now he saw that she really had been hesitant to flee from the outlaw stronghold. A part of her *wanted* to stay here with Lobo.

And from the familiar way he had spoken to her, it was obvious that Lobo and Juliana had known each other before the raid on the mustang camp. That at least partially explained some of the things that had puzzled Fargo, such as why Lobo had left the Barrientos family alone for so long.

But there were other questions to be answered, like the exact nature of the relationship between Juliana Barrientos and the bandit chief, and why Lobo's behavior had changed so abruptly, leading him to attack the Barrientos family.

Fargo didn't have time to speculate on any of this, because even as the thoughts flashed through his brain, his captors began to hustle him toward the house. Lobo and Juliana followed along behind. Lobo kept the heavy pistol in his hand.

As Fargo was shoved roughly through the door into the main room, he got a chance to look at it. He had freed Elena from her captivity in this room, but had been too busy doing that to pay much attention to his surroundings. He saw now that Lobo's apparent fondness for finery extended to this room as well. The furniture was heavy and overstuffed, there were thick rugs scattered about on the floor, and the room was lit by, of all things, a crystal chandelier that hung from the ceiling. To see such a thing in the middle of this thorny wilderness was little short of amazing.

Something else caught Fargo's eye. On the wall over the fireplace hung two crossed swords, heavy cutlasses with curved hilts that looked like gold. On the opposite wall was an ancient musket, flanked by a pair of equally old flintlock pistols. Fargo had to wonder where the weapons had come from and what their significance was to Johnny Lobo.

"Put him in the chair," Lobo ordered his men, motioning toward the same chair where Elena had been tied. The outlaws thrust him down and then, at Lobo's command, they tied his arms to the arms of the chair. They left Fargo's legs free, but he couldn't stand up without taking the heavy piece of furniture with him.

Once that was done, Lobo ordered the men to go back outside and help the others bring the mustangs back under control. "We'll be shorthanded now," Lobo added with a bitter, angry look at Fargo. "We must have lost at least half a dozen men during this disturbance."

Now that Fargo had heard Lobo's voice several more times, he was finally able to determine that the man's accent was British. It had faded somewhat with time, which made it less distinctive. Lobo must have been away from England for quite a while, but Fargo figured he had been born and raised there. Quite a few Englishmen had immigrated to the American frontier, and Fargo had run into his share of them.

When the other outlaws left, Fargo was alone with Lobo and Juliana. Juliana kept her eyes fixed on the floor, obviously unwilling to meet Fargo's gaze. Lobo didn't mind, though. He tucked the pistol behind his belt, parked his considerable bulk right in front of the chair, and glared down at Fargo. "It's about time we met face-to-face, you hell-raisin' bastard," Lobo declared.

"We've crossed trails a couple of times," Fargo replied.

Lobo nodded. "Aye, you gave us a merry scamper through the chaparral. I wanted that stallion you were on. Fine-lookin' piece of horseflesh, that one. Where is he now?"

Fargo didn't say anything, and after a moment Lobo chuckled.

"Won't give him up, eh? Can't say as I blame you. If I had a horse like that, I wouldn't want to lose him, either. Of course in your case it doesn't really matter, because you're going to die regardless."

Juliana finally lifted her head. "No, John," she said. "There's no need to kill him, is there?"

Lobo turned toward her. "I'm sorry, m'love. He knows where this place is. We can't allow him to live. He's too big a threat to us. The lads wouldn't allow it."

"You are their leader. They will allow what you tell them to allow."

"Most of the time. But when it comes to keepin' their hideout safe . . ." Lobo shrugged his massive shoulders. "I can't go against them on that."

"What about Elena? Would you have her killed, too, to protect the sanctity of this place?"

Lobo looked stricken. "Of course not! I could never harm any of your flesh and blood, Juliana."

"You certainly tried," she shot back, with a semblance of her old spirit flashing in her eyes and voice. "You attacked our camp not once but twice."

"And I gave the men strict orders that none of the girls were to be harmed."

"What about my husband? He was harmed. I saw him shot."

Lobo's face hardened. "He had it comin' to him, the damned thief."

"Eduardo never stole anything from you!"

Lobo stepped over to her and grasped her arms, pulling her against him. "Just the thing that I held dearest in all the world," he said.

Juliana couldn't pull away from his overpowering grip, but she turned her head so that she wasn't looking at him. Lobo stood there for a moment, holding her like that, before he let her go and stepped back

117

with a growl deep in his throat. He turned back toward Fargo, his scowl and his huge hairy form making him look a little like a grizzly bear.

"We haven't been properly introduced, sir," he said. "My name is John Wolfe. And you are . . . ?"

"Skye Fargo. I reckon I see now why you call yourself Johnny Lobo."

The big man's teeth flashed in the dark, tangled beard. "You speak the Spanish tongue?"

"Enough to know that lobo means wolf."

"How about French? Do you know what a *boucanier* is?"

"A pirate," Fargo said flatly. "That's where the word buccaneer comes from."

"Aye." Lobo swept a big hand toward the door. "And out there is my band of buccaneers. Pirates on horseback. Scourge of the Nueces country, instead of the seven seas."

Fargo wondered briefly if the man was at least partially mad. Whatever Lobo's mental state might be, Fargo wanted to keep him talking. The longer Lobo waited before sending his men after Elena and Rooster, the better the chances that the two of them would get away.

"How did a buccaneer come to be up here, so far away from the ocean?"

"Not so far, really. As long as royal ships loaded with riches have sailed the waters of the Gulf of Mexico, there have been pirates willing to risk all for plunder, just like in the Caribbean. Why, old Jean Lafitte amassed a fortune in treasure taken from ships in the gulf."

Fargo had run into folks looking for Jean Lafitte's treasure over close to Galveston, so he knew quite a bit about pirate loot and the lure it held for greedy men. He said, "So you tried to imitate Lafitte, did you?"

Lobo snorted. "Johnny Lobo is no mere imitation! I was feared from one end of the gulf to the other in my time." He waved toward the crossed cutlasses, and the old musket and pistols. "Those are mementoes from those days, keepsakes I picked up in the islands. They date from the time of Cap'n Edward Teach and that lot. I was one of 'em, a latter-day Blackbeard! And nobody knew that John Wolfe, the English gentleman, was also the bloody-handed pirate Johnny Lobo!"

"What happened?" Fargo asked. "Why did you give it up?"

Lobo looked over at Juliana. "I met a woman," he said, his voice softening a little. "A beautiful young woman who lived in Veracruz, the daughter of a Spanish diplomat. A woman for whom I would have given up anything. . . ."

"But then she went off to Mexico City and married another man," Fargo said.

"Aye! That left me with no choice but to return to the sea."

"Back to a life of piracy."

Lobo nodded and raised a clenched fist. "I made the Spaniards pay, and the Mexicans, too! I'd be there still if not for the day that a damned Spanish ship sunk my vessel out from under me. The *Juliana* went to the bottom, and all hands with her, save for me. I was able to grab a piece of wreckage and floated with it for three days before I finally washed ashore. Many's the time that sharks bumped my legs during those long days and nights, but the Lord's grace protected me. None of the creatures decided to take a bite out of my hide." Lobo lowered his arm. "By the time I came ashore, I knew I'd had enough of the sea. I made my way to a place where I'd cached extra gear and some of my loot. That was enough to buy me clothes and a horse and some guns. I made my way inland and found men hiding here in the brasada, men on the run from the law. It didn't take me long to mold them into the sort of crew that I wanted."

"I met Father Pascual in Dinero," Fargo said. "He showed me one of the old Spanish coins you gave him to help feed the poor. You told him they didn't have any blood on them. That was a lie, wasn't it? Those coins were part of your loot."

Lobo gave a short bark of humorless laughter. "You think a child's empty belly knows whether or not there's blood on a coin? If it buys a loaf of bread to fill that belly, do you think the child cares?" He made a slashing motion with his hand. "I told the padre what he needed to hear so that he could put the money to good use. You see, Fargo, when I was drifting out there in the gulf, holdin' on to that spar for dear life and feeling the sharks brush against my legs, I made a bargain with the Lord. Get me to shore alive, I said, and when I get there I'll do some good for folks who need it."

"You're an outlaw!" Fargo burst out. "You rob and kill!"

A smile twisted Lobo's lips. "I never promised the Lord that I'd do *all* good. Just some."

Fargo looked over at Juliana, who was gazing at the floor again. "When did you discover that Señora Barrientos and her family were up here in this area, too?"

The smile, perverse though it was, disappeared from Lobo's face and was replaced once more by a scowl. "Don't call her that!" he snapped. "As for when I found her again, it was only a short time. I believe we were drawn together, the same as we always were. But even though I hated Eduardo, I decided to leave them alone. For old time's sake, I suppose you could say."

"What about Rooster Jones? He said you never bothered him, either."

"The old man who hauls cotton through these parts? He reminded me of old Elihu Dobbs, the cap'n who took me under his wing long ago, when I was just a lad, an indentured servant shipped off to the Bahamas. Call me a sentimental fool, but I didn't want to hurt the old man because of that. Of course, when he fell in with you, that changed everything."

"What changed your attitude toward the Barrientos family? Why did you suddenly attack them?"

Lobo began to pace. "A man's heart can only stand so much torment. Many's the night I sat my horse, out in the brush, watching their camp. Seeing dear Juliana there, so close and yet still out of reach. Seeing the children, those beautiful girls . . . the girls that should have been ours, mine and hers, not hers and Eduardo's!" He flung his arms wide. "Then finally the night came when I could withstand the torment no longer! I knew that if they stayed, Juliana had to be mine again."

A few feet away, Juliana lifted her hands and covered her face with them. She didn't cry, but a shudder ran through her.

"But I couldn't just steal her away, Fargo," Lobo went on. "Lord knows why I feel 'tis important that you understand me, unless it's because I sense that we're alike in many ways, you and I."

Fargo could have argued with that—he didn't think he was anything like this bloodthirsty former pirate and current bandit leader—but he decided it would be better to remain silent and let Lobo continue with his rambling rant. Every minute that passed was another minute that Elena and Rooster could put some distance between themselves and the outlaw stronghold, Fargo hoped.

"So instead of just taking her, I thought that perhaps an attack would drive them from the brasada," Lobo said. "I hoped that Eduardo would give up mustangin' and go somewhere else, somewhere I wouldn't have to see Juliana and be tortured by the knowledge that she was close by. I wasn't really tryin' to steal those wild horses. That's why I broke the attack off so quick when you and the two girls came riding up." Lobo shook his great, shaggy head. "Of course, it didn't work. It just made Eduardo more stubborn than ever, more determined to stay and work with those mustangs. Then I knew what I must do. I had to kill him and reclaim what was rightfully mine."

Juliana lowered her hands and said, "Eduardo never harmed you, John! I never even met him until after you and I had parted. He had nothing to do with my refusal to stay in Veracruz with you."

"You can say what you want, m'love, but I know better. Eduardo Barrientos doomed himself by takin' your love away from me, and I'll not feel sorry for him now."

Juliana covered her face again, and this time she began to cry. Lobo went to her and tried to put his arms around her to comfort her, but she pulled away from him. He let her go, and she turned and ran out of the room, into the bedroom. The door slammed behind her.

Lobo looked at the closed door, shook his head, and gave a long, heavy sigh. "Love is a terrible thing, Fargo," he said. "Sometimes I think it keeps people apart as much as it brings them together. And yet none of us can live without it."

Fargo wasn't in much of a mood to listen to this

brigand's half-baked philosophy. He said, "Why attack tonight? Why did you wait?"

Lobo's eyes glittered with hatred as he looked at the Trailsman. "Ah, that was because of *you*, Fargo."

"Me?" The exclamation was startled out of him.

"Aye. I had a score to settle with you. First you killed one of my men when we tried to take that fine horse away from you, and then later you murdered Sanderson and DeWalt, down in Dinero."

"That wasn't murder," Fargo said angrily. "It was self-defense. They were trying to kill me, and they could have killed a bunch of innocent people by starting that fire."

"I know, I know," Lobo said with a wave of his hand. "They were impulsive lads. Hector told me all about it. But that doesn't absolve you of your guilt."

"So anybody who gets in the way of you or your men deserves whatever happens to them. Is that it?"

"Johnny Lobo is like a force of nature, lad. You can't blame a hurricane for blowing, now can you?"

Fargo's jaw tightened with disgust, and he didn't bother trying to conceal the reaction. "I've run up against plenty of no-good owlhoots in my time, Lobo. You're just another one of them, murdering scum who's always ready to blame somebody else for the suffering he causes!"

Lobo's eyes narrowed to slits, and his hand went to the butt of the gun behind his belt. "That's mighty big talk for a man who's trussed up as helpless as a kitten."

"Untie me, then, and we can settle it between us. You waited until I was close to the Barrientos camp because you wanted me to come after you, didn't you?"

"Aye, I had it in mind!" Lobo admitted. "I had men watchin' the trail between Dinero and the camp, and when they reported that you and the girl would be there soon, I knew the time had come to strike! I figured you'd come after us, and then I'd have you where I wanted you, right in the palm of my hand!"

The man ought to call himself Johnny *Loco*, Fargo thought, because he was definitely crazy.

Not stupid, though. Lobo had manipulated things just like he wanted, and now he had not only Juliana in his power, but also Fargo.

"Why did you kidnap Elena, too? I thought it was just Juliana you wanted."

"I thought it might make her happy to have one of her girls with her," Lobo said casually, "so when the opportunity was there to grab Elena, too, I took it." He paused, and then added meaningfully, "And don't think you're foolin' me, Fargo. I know what you're tryin' to do. You think by keeping me talkin', you're givin' the girl more time to get away. But I'm not worried about that. It'll take her some time to make her way through the chaparral, and she won't get far on foot. I'll send some men out in a few minutes, and she'll be rounded up and brought back here by mornin'."

Fargo felt a surge of hope at Lobo's overconfident words. The man didn't realize that he'd had help, that Rooster Jones had come with him to this hideout buried deep in the chaparral. Lobo had been unconscious when Rooster started shooting and yelling to stampede the mustangs. He didn't know that Fargo and Rooster had left their horses outside the thicket. With any luck, Elena wasn't on foot at all.

"I thought Juliana was confused at first, when I tried to rescue her, and I guess she was," Fargo said. "She wasn't sure whether she wanted to get away from you or not."

Lobo's bearded jaw jutted out. "She loves me still!"

he declared. "After all these years, her feelin's for me are as strong as ever!"

Fargo doubted that, considering how Juliana had acted during Lobo's rambling discourse, but there was a kernel of truth to it. Juliana *did* have some feelings left for the man she had known as John Wolfe. Some lingering fondness, a nostalgic sense of what might have been if only things were different, a reluctance to hurt a man she had once loved . . . add them all up and Juliana truly was confused.

In the end, though, Fargo felt certain that she really loved her husband, and she would never be happy living with the man who had, for all she knew, killed Eduardo. In his maniacal obsession, Lobo couldn't see that he would never have what he really wanted. He would never have Juliana's heart. That hope had sunk as surely as the seagoing vessel Lobo had named after her.

A knock sounded on the door of the house. Lobo swung toward it and growled, "What?"

Hector Rios opened the door and stepped into the room. He cast a hate-filled glance at Fargo, then said, "We have eight men dead, Capitán, and three more hurt so bad they are no good to us. But the mustangs are back under control. We have them grazing on the other side of the resaca, as before."

"Almost half our forces dead or injured," Lobo muttered with a grimace. He looked at Fargo. "This man has a great deal to pay for. Do you know why the mustangs stampeded like they did?"

Rios frowned. "Capitán . . . it was the other man who caused the stampede. The one who came with this one."

Lobo's head lifted sharply. "The other man?" he repeated. "What other man?"

"The old viejo . . . the one called Rooster."

Lobo turned sharply toward Fargo. "Rooster was with you? You had horses?"

Fargo just smiled. Lobo was beginning to realize that Elena might not be so easy to catch after all.

With a snarl, Lobo swung his treelike arm and slammed a blow across Fargo's face. The impact jerked Fargo's head to the side, and made lightning flash behind his eyes and thunder roar inside his skull, but he didn't lose consciousness. Feeling a trickle of blood from his mouth, he looked up at Lobo and smiled again. Maybe if he could goad Lobo into knocking him over, one of the chair arms might break, and then Fargo could get at least one hand free. . . .

It was the slimmest of hopes, and Lobo denied him even that by stepping back, his chest heaving with rage as he glowered at Fargo. After a couple of seconds as he struggled to control himself, he turned his head and said to Rios, "Get some of the men and go look for that girl—*now!*"

"*Sí,* Capitán." With a glance toward Fargo that was almost pitying, Rios hurried out of the room. Maybe Rios knew that whatever vengeance Lobo took on his prisoner, it would be terrible.

"You had better hope that they find her, Fargo," Lobo said in a low, dangerous tone. "If they do, maybe I'll kill you quick. If they don't . . ."

He didn't have to finish his sentence. Fargo didn't know exactly what Lobo had in mind—but he sure as hell got the general idea.

Lobo left Fargo alone then and went into the bedroom. Fargo strained against his bonds, anger giving him strength as he thought about what the madman might be doing to Juliana Barrientos, but even so, he was unable to budge the cruel knots that held him down. He looked around the room for something he

126

might be able to use to cut himself free. His eyes lit on the crossed cutlasses above the fireplace, and for a second he felt a surge of hope.

It vanished quickly, though, when he realized that even if he could drag the heavy chair that far—something that might not even be possible—he still couldn't get to the cutlasses. They were much too high for him to reach while he was tied into the chair. There was nothing he could use to knock them off their pegs so that they might fall within his reach, either.

He sagged back, struggling against a feeling of despair. It was not in Skye Fargo's nature to give up, no matter how bleak things might look. He figured that as long as he was drawing breath, he still had a chance to fight back and turn the odds in his favor. Victory would never be completely out of his grasp until he was dead.

But sometimes a fella had to just sit back and bide his time, and it looked like this was one of those occasions. His breath hissed between his clenched teeth in an angry sigh.

All right, he told himself, if that was the way it was, he would just rest for a while and conserve his strength until he had a chance to use it.

He didn't hear any yelling or crying from inside the other room, although from time to time he could make out the soft sound of voices from in there. Lobo was probably trying to talk Juliana around to seeing things his way. If that was the case, he must have failed, because when he came out a little while later, he still looked angry and frustrated. With a glare at Fargo, he went out of the house, slamming the front door behind him.

Fargo's head turned toward the bedroom door. He waited to see if Juliana was going to come out. If she did, maybe he could talk her into cutting him loose, even though it would mean going against Lobo, something she seemed reluctant to do even though she wasn't really going to cooperate with him, either.

She didn't come out, and if she heard Fargo's hissed call of "Señora Barrientos!", she didn't respond to it.

Finally, exhaustion claimed Fargo. His head sagged against the high back of the chair that had become his prison. He dozed off.

When the door was kicked open an unknowable time later and Lobo strode into the room, Fargo looked past the big man and saw dawn light spreading across the clearing in the chaparral. Lobo came directly to Fargo and caught hold of his chin, digging fingers in cruelly as he wrenched Fargo's head up and glared down at him with blazing eyes.

"Rios and the others couldn't find her," Lobo said. "She got away, damn you! Her and the old man both! Now it'll be that much harder to make Juliana love me again."

Juliana would never love him again, but Fargo didn't see any point in saying that. Lobo was already mad enough without rubbing salt in his emotional wounds.

"It's time for you to pay for what you've done," Lobo went on. Hector Rios and a couple of other men had come into the room behind him. He turned to them and gestured at Fargo. "Take him."

Juliana must have been listening at the bedroom door. She jerked it open and rushed out, catching hold of Lobo's arm. "Please, John, no!" she said. "No more killing. Please."

He looked down at her, his face stony. "You don't understand," he said. "You never understood. If a man's to be strong, he can't allow his enemies to defy him. Fargo has to pay." He nodded to Rios and the others.

Juliana began to cry as Rios pulled a knife and stepped toward the chair. Instead of using the knife on Fargo, he cut the ropes holding the Trailsman. The other men grabbed Fargo's arms and jerked him to his feet. During the night, Fargo's hands had gone numb from the tightness of the bonds, and now pain jabbed them mercilessly as the blood began to flow again.

"Take him out," Lobo growled.

Rios sheathed his knife and drew his gun, just in case Fargo tried to fight. After the long hours of captivity, Fargo was in no shape to do that. The outlaws forced him to the door and then outside the house. The sound of Juliana's sobbing dwindled behind him.

Lobo must have given his men precise orders. A bandanna was whipped around Fargo's eyes and tied in place. He was lifted onto a horse and his hands were tied together, and then he was lashed to the saddle. Momentarily blind and helpless, he felt the mount move under him as the horse was led away from the outlaw stronghold. The occasional prick of a thorn told him that he was being taken through the chaparral. The trail twisted and turned, but he couldn't tell if it was the same one he and Rooster had followed to the outlaw camp the night before.

Finally, Rios announced, "Here," and Fargo's horse was brought to a halt. He felt the rope holding him to the saddle part under the stroke of a knife. A sudden hard shove sent him toppling off the horse. Instinctively, he put out his hands to break his fall, and agonizing pain lanced into them as he landed on what felt like a clump of prickly pear cactus. He rolled away, but not before his hands were on fire from the needles embedded in his palms.

Rios and the other men laughed. The segundo said, "Take his clothes."

Fargo was lifted to his feet, and then he felt hands tugging at his buckskins. Ignoring the pain, he clasped his bound hands together and swung them like a club, trying to fight back. He struck something yielding, and a man grunted in pain and then cursed.

"Damn it, Clark, don't you shoot him!" Rios said. "You know what El Capitán's orders were."

"Yeah, yeah," muttered the man Fargo had struck. "I can bust the son of a bitch in the mouth, can't I?"

"Yeah, go ahead. Might make him more cooperative."

With that warning, Fargo tried to jerk his head out of the way, but he was too late. A fist smashed into his mouth and knocked him sprawling on his back. He heard a knife blade ripping through his buckskins while he was half stunned, and in a matter of a couple of minutes, his clothing had been cut and torn off of his body. He was left lying naked in the dust, his aching hands still bound and the blindfold still over his eyes.

"All right, Fargo, we'll say adios now." Rios's tone was mocking. "El Capitán said to leave you a little present to help you enjoy your stay in the chaparral. It's that big knife of yours. We'll leave it down the trail a ways."

With that, the men spurred their horses. Fargo heard the hoofbeats receding as he lay there trying to catch his breath. He was a little surprised the outlaws hadn't just gone ahead and killed him. That wouldn't have been cruel enough to satisfy Lobo, though. The man had something even worse in mind.

Fargo's hands hurt like blazes. He wanted to get the cactus needles out of them. First, though, he had to see what he was doing. Though his hands were lashed together, he was able to lift them to his head and try to push the bandanna up with his thumbs to get it away from his eyes. It was tied tightly, though, and didn't want to move. Fargo kept working at it until gradually he began to see a strip of light along the lower edge of the blindfold.

He paused in the effort when suddenly he heard something. It wasn't the hoofbeats of the horses returning. Rather it was a crackling and crashing in the brush somewhere not far off. A moment later, Fargo heard something else that made the blood in his veins turn to ice.

He heard the grunting of a javelina, and from the deep-chested power of it and the noise of the creature moving through the chaparral, Fargo could tell that the beast was huge, one of those freaks of nature that were sometimes found here in the brasada.

And since the sounds were getting louder, he knew that the monster was coming straight at him.

9

Naked, unarmed, blindfolded, hands tied together and full of stinging cactus needles, and now a wild, razor-tusked hog big enough to gobble him up by itself was rumbling through the brush toward him. A man might think that at least things couldn't get any worse.

Fargo knew better than to think that.

Things could always get worse.

But he wasn't ready to give up yet, either. The javelina was coming closer, but it wasn't here yet. Fargo resumed his efforts to push the blindfold off his head, but there was some added urgency in his movements now.

A minute later the blindfold came loose and he could see again. He looked around, trying to spot the Arkansas toothpick. Rios had said they were leaving it for him to find, but the outlaw segundo could have been lying about that. If Fargo could reach the knife, he could cut himself loose and at least be able to fight back if the beast attacked him.

The Arkansas toothpick was nowhere to be seen.

Fargo bit back a curse. He was lying in a very small clearing in the chaparral. Several narrow trails converged on it. This was someplace he hadn't been before, he sensed. He had no idea where Lobo's hideout was from here. Not that it would matter unless he could get free and somehow escape from that javelina, he reminded himself.

He rolled over and pulled himself into a sitting position. Lifting his wrists to his mouth, he began pulling at the ropes with his teeth. He wanted to stop and pull the stickers from his hands, but it was more important to get loose. As he worked at the bonds, he listened to the snuffling and grunting from the javelina. Maybe the creature hadn't smelled him yet. It didn't seem to be in any real hurry to get to him.

Fargo tasted blood in his mouth as he tore at the ropes, trying to loosen them. The outlaws had done a good job of tying him. Finally one strand parted, then another, and after that it went a little faster. After what seemed like an eternity to Fargo, the ropes fell free around his wrists.

He stood up. The bastards had even taken his boots. Standing there for a moment, dizziness made his head spin. When it settled down a little, he looked at the trails branching off from the clearing and bit back a curse. There were hoofprints leading in and out on all of them, obviously put there by Lobo's men to confuse him. He began to trudge along a trail that led in the direction away from the sounds made by the giant javelina, hoping it was the right one. As he walked, Fargo used his teeth again to pluck the needles from his hands, being careful to spit them out.

Would he find his knife along this trail? He didn't know. But one path was as good as any when he had no idea where he was or how to get out of this thorny, trackless wilderness.

The trail began to grow even more narrow. Briars and brambles caught at him, raking his bare flesh, leaving thin lines of slowly oozing red on his skin. Fargo had finally gotten all the needles picked out of his hands when the path suddenly came to an end. The mesquites and the other man-killing plants closed in.

Fargo had no choice but to turn around and go back the way he had come, even though it meant he would be heading toward the javelina that still stalked through the brush.

Blood seeped from the multitude of wounds on his hands and trickled down to form drops of crimson on his fingertips. He shook them off and tried to will himself to ignore the pain. When he reached the clearing where he had been left by the outlaws, he picked one of the other trails and started along it.

Within minutes, the sounds in the brush abruptly shifted direction and started coming closer to him. The grunting became louder and more urgent. Fargo knew that the javelina had finally caught his scent and was now seeking him out, taking the shortest route through the chaparral because the creature's thick hide was like armor.

Fargo began moving faster, too, trotting along the trail. He went around a bend. The crashing in the brush was off to his left as he entered a stretch of the path that ran fairly straight for forty or fifty yards. He paused just for an instant as he spotted the Arkansas toothpick lying in the trail just this side of the next turn. Then he ran even harder toward the knife.

He was less than halfway there when the javelina burst out of the thicket into the trail behind him. The grunting was obscenely loud now as the bristle-backed porker swung his razor-tusked snout toward Fargo. The javelina lumbered into a surprisingly swift run.

Fargo glanced over his shoulder and saw the beast

barreling down on him like a runaway train. The javelina was about three feet tall and five feet long, several times larger than usual, and probably weighed at least four hundred pounds. There had to be at least one domestic hog in his ancestry for him to have achieved that size.

Fargo didn't care about the javelina's family tree. He just wanted to stay ahead of the blasted thing. He sprinted for the knife, not looking back again. He didn't have to look to know that the javelina was gaining on him.

Fargo's bare feet slapped the dirt of the path. The javelina was so close behind him that he could feel the heat of its breath on his legs, like flame from the snout of some fire-breathing dragon in an old fairy-tale book. He threw himself forward in a rolling dive, slapping at the handle of the Arkansas toothpick as he twisted aside. He wound up in the edge of the brush, where thorns clawed and tore at his skin.

But the javelina, although surprisingly light on its feet, was going too fast to turn and thundered past Fargo. As the giant beast went by him, Fargo thrust the blade into its side. The javelina let out an outraged squeal of pain.

Fargo's hand was slick with blood, but he managed to hang on to the knife. He pushed himself up, threw a leg over the back of the javelina, and cried out in pain himself as the bristles on the animal's back raked and scraped at his bare skin. Fargo looped his right arm around the javelina's neck and held on tightly while he ripped the knife free and plunged the blade back in, again and again. The javelina whirled around and around, trying to reach the thing on its back that was inflicting so much pain on it. Blood sprayed through the air in a grisly shower.

Fargo slammed the knife into the javelina again.

The squealing beast just wanted to get away now. It slammed into the wall of brush. Fargo screamed as thorns ripped into him. He tore the knife free and more blood burst hotly from the giant javelina's side. Letting go, Fargo slid off the animal's back and fell to the ground in the underbrush. He was only half conscious, but he held on to the knife. Instinct commanded him not to let go of it.

Vaguely, he heard the wounded javelina crash through the chaparral for a few more yards. Then the sound stopped, and when Fargo forced himself to lift his head and look, he saw that the beast had halted and fallen down on its forelegs. With a rumbling sigh, it toppled over on its side. The great barrel of its chest rose and fell a few more times, and then death claimed the animal.

Fargo's face, covered with blood from what felt like a million cuts and scratches, stretched painfully into a grin of triumph. The beast was dead—*and the man was still alive.*

The victory would mean nothing, though, if Fargo didn't get out of here. He couldn't just lie in this thorny tangle. Although every movement brought more cuts and fresh pain, he struggled to turn around and crawl back toward the trail.

For a moment there, at the height of the battle with the javelina, he had been little better than a wild beast himself, living only to kill his enemy. But now rational thought was coming back to him and he remembered Johnny Lobo and the Barrientos family and the outlaw stronghold in the middle of the chaparral. Since Rios had dropped the knife, it meant that this trail led out of the brush. All Fargo had to do was follow it.

He wondered if Rios and the others had known about the javelina when they left him here. Such a terrible beast was probably infamous in these parts, and the outlaws easily could have been aware that the monster frequented this area. That was Lobo's revenge, leaving Fargo out here to run afoul of the creature.

And yet, Lobo had instructed Rios to leave the knife—to give the Trailsman a fighting chance? That struck Fargo as something Lobo's twisted personality would do.

Lobo was going to be sorry, Fargo thought as he pulled himself along painfully through the underbrush. Sure, he was still naked, smeared and splattered with blood, covered with cuts and scrapes and bruises, and in so much pain that he wanted to scream . . .

But he was alive, and Lobo was going to be sorry.

That was Fargo's last thought as he emerged from the brush, collapsed on the trail, and passed out.

Gnawing hunger and incredible thirst woke him. Fargo had no idea how long he had been unconscious, but he figured it had been quite a while. He was too stiff and sore to move, or even to lift his head. Eventually he was able to open his eyes, though.

The light in the chaparral was dim. That didn't tell him anything. It was always dim in this wasteland, except when the sun was directly overhead. He might have been out for an hour, or all day.

He flexed his fingers first. That cracked the dried blood on his hands. He moved his toes and then stretched his legs. The muscles in his shoulders bunched. He put his hands flat on the ground and pushed. His body came up a little. It worked. Everything worked. Relief flooded through Fargo. If he could just get something to eat and drink, he would be all right. Maybe find someplace where he could slip down in a tub full of hot water and soak all the dried blood off his skin while the heat eased his aches and pains.

The only problem with that idea was that the nearest tub of hot water was probably in Corpus Christi, and that was at least a two-day ride away. And he didn't have a horse anymore. Or any clothes.

He started to laugh.

The laughter died away as he thought about Johnny Lobo and Juliana Barrientos. Juliana was still Lobo's prisoner. He had to get back there somehow and try to help her, whether she wanted his help or not.

Fargo pushed himself onto hands and knees. It looked like he might have to crawl there.

That was when he heard the slow, measured thud of a horse's hooves coming along the trail.

Fargo tensed. It was unlikely that anybody riding along this trail would be a friend. More than likely the rider was one of the outlaws, returning to make sure he was dead. Lobo might enjoy toying with Fargo, making it look like he had a fighting chance to survive, but in the end, Lobo wanted him dead. The rider might even be the massive bandit chief himself, come to check on Fargo.

His head swiveling from side to side, Fargo looked for someplace to hide. There wasn't any. He wasn't going to crawl into that thorny hellhole again.

The hoofbeats were close now, right around the bend in the trail.

Fargo did the only thing he could. He stretched out facedown in the trail and lay motionless with his right arm underneath his body. In his right hand he clutched the Arkansas toothpick.

He took a deep breath and held it, willing himself to be absolutely still. Naked, with blood smeared all over him, he probably looked dead as dead could be. He had to hope that whoever was riding along the trail would think so and decide not to waste a bullet on him.

If the rider was one of the other outlaws and not Lobo himself, the man probably had orders to find Fargo's body and bring it back to the hideout. Lobo would want to see for himself that Fargo was dead. That would mean the man would have to dismount and sling the corpse over the back of his horse. Fargo hoped desperately that was the case.

The hoofbeats came around the bend in the trail and stopped. Fargo didn't budge. After a moment, Hector Rios' voice said, "Ah, muchacho, you look awful! You must have panicked and tried to escape through the chaparral. Ah, well, at least El Gordo did not get you. Consider yourself lucky. Being eaten alive by that one is no way to go."

For one harrowing second, Fargo had thought that Rios realized he was still alive. Then he decided that the outlaw segundo was just talking idly to what he believed to be a dead man. El Gordo had to be that giant javelina. Fargo's guess had been right—the beast *was* famous around these parts.

Fargo heard saddle leather creak as Rios dismounted. The air in his lungs was running out and he really needed to take another breath. But he remained motionless as Rios' footsteps approached. The dust kicked up by the man's boots tickled Fargo's nose. He resisted the urge to sneeze.

"El Capitán wants to see you, muchacho," Rios went on, and from the sound of his voice Fargo knew the man was right above him now. "He will not rest until he knows you are dead. But he does not want the señora to see you, no. That would not be good."

Because Lobo didn't want Juliana to know just how crazed with hate he really was, thought Fargo. As if she didn't already realize that. . . .

"Damn, I never seen an hombre so scratched up," Rios said. He took hold of Fargo's shoulders. Fargo willed his muscles to remain limp. With a grunt of effort, Rios rolled him over.

Fargo thrust up with the knife, burying it to the hilt in the Mexican's stomach.

Rios' mouth opened and his eyes bulged. He made an incoherent noise. Still bent over, as he had been when he rolled Fargo onto his back, Rios clawed at the revolver on his hip.

Fargo pulled down on the knife, opening a huge wound in Rios' midsection. The man's guts sagged out. His knees unhinged and he fell. Fargo pushed him aside and ripped with the knife. Rios made a gurgling noise and stiffened. He hadn't been able to draw his gun before dying.

Killing the man had taken just about all of Fargo's strength. He pulled the knife free and rolled onto his back. His chest heaved up and down as he tried to catch his breath.

After several minutes, Fargo was able to sit up. He unbuckled Rios' gun belt and pulled it off the man. Then he went to work on Rios' boots. The sombrero had fallen off and rolled to one side when Rios collapsed, so it was well away from the pool of blood forming around the body. Once Fargo had Rios' boots off, he tugged the tight trousers down the man's legs. They had some blood on them, but they weren't sodden and ruined the way Rios' shirt and charro jacket were. That was lucky, because Fargo had to have some clothes for what he was going to do next. He couldn't ride into the outlaw camp naked.

Moving slowly to conserve his strength, Fargo got

dressed in Rios' trousers and boots. They were a little tight, but Rios had been almost as big as Fargo, so they were comfortable enough—as comfortable as any dead man's clothes could be. He buckled on the gun belt and slid the revolver out of its leather. It was a similar model to Fargo's Colt, and he knew he wouldn't have any trouble using it. He holstered the gun and then tucked the Arkansas toothpick behind the belt.

Rios' horse was skittish, but Fargo's quiet voice soon soothed the animal. Fargo was able to come up to the horse and check the rolled-up pack behind the saddle. He found a serape in there and put his head through the opening, draping the colorful garment over his shoulders. That would conceal the fact that he wasn't wearing a shirt. Finally, he picked up the sombrero and put it on his head. The little decorative balls dangling from the brim swayed in front of his eyes and made him frown. That would be damned distracting in a gunfight.

Fortunately, he didn't intend to be wearing the broad-brimmed hat for very long. He just needed it to get him back into the camp. If he kept his head down, he thought he could make it all the way to Lobo's house. It made sense that Rios would go there to report to his "El Capitán" when he returned from his errand in the chaparral.

A wave of weakness and dizziness swept abruptly over Fargo. He held on to the saddle to steady himself until it passed. He had lost a lot of blood, and it had been well over a day since he'd had anything to eat or drink. A look at the sky told him it was late afternoon. He had been unconscious for most of the day.

Rios had a bottle of tequila in his saddlebags. Fargo uncorked it and took a swig of the fiery liquor. It burned all the way down and hit his belly like a keg of blasting powder going off. But at least his mouth wasn't so dry anymore. Fargo dug deeper in the saddlebags and found a couple of stale tortillas. He wolfed them down, knowing he needed something in his stomach to soak up some of that tequila. Nausea made his belly clench as he ate, but he got the tortillas down, and a few minutes later he began to feel a little better.

When he thought he could manage it without falling down, he put a foot in the stirrup and swung up onto the horse. It danced around a little underneath him until Fargo tightened the reins and said firmly, "That's enough." He turned the horse and heeled it into a walk, heading back along the trail in the direction Rios had come from, leaving the man's body crumpled in the path behind him.

The trail serpentined its way through the chaparral for at least a mile before it merged with another trail. Fargo picked out the hoofprints of Rios' horse and followed them. He didn't hurry. The sun wasn't quite down yet, and he figured it would be better if he didn't try to enter the outlaw camp until after dark.

The trail left the chaparral, and Fargo reined in with a frown as he looked at the mile-wide stretch of open ground before him. He had to find the brushy area where the clearing that contained the outlaw hideout was located, and the only way to do that was to continue backtracking Hector Rios. Now the fading light gave Fargo an added sense of urgency. By this time he knew the tracks that Rios' horse had left, but following them in the gathering dusk might be difficult.

All he could do was try. He set out across the open ground, hoping no one was watching. Rios would have known where he was going, and Fargo didn't want his tentativeness to give away the masquerade.

The skills he had acquired during his adventurous

life now came in handy yet again. A hoofprint, a broken branch, a clump of bent-over grass slowly rising upright again . . . all those things and more Fargo's keen eyes picked out, and he was able to cross the open area fairly quickly. As he neared another wall of brush, he recognized it as the one he and Rooster had approached the night before. When he got there and picked out the hoofprints of the stolen mustangs in the last of the light, he knew he was in the right place. He wasn't going to get lost now.

Fargo rode slowly along the winding trail. He began to smell smoke, just like on the previous night, and knew the gang had built a fire again. When he reached the edge of the clearing, he saw the flames leaping in the air. There were fewer men gathered around the fire tonight, though.

And there were several graves over to the side of the clearing, an indication of the bloody work Fargo and Rooster had done.

Fargo walked the horse toward Lobo's house, keeping his head down as he rode. Some of the men by the fire called out to him, thinking he was Rios. Fargo just grunted and raised a hand as if in greeting, but he kept moving toward Lobo's house. The outlaws didn't seem to think there was anything unusual about that. After all, Rios was Lobo's segundo. It made sense that he would go and report to the boss when he rode in.

When he reached the house, he reined in and stiffly dismounted. Fargo had only a rough plan. He would get into the house, put his gun—well, Rios' gun—to Lobo's head, and force the man to leave the hideout. At gunpoint, Fargo would take Lobo and Juliana out of here, and the rest of the gang wouldn't dare pursue them as long as their leader's life was at risk. At least, that was the way Fargo hoped things would play out.

He would need a considerable amount of luck to pull this off, of course. And he wasn't sure how long he could force his tortured, exhausted body to keep working. Even now, keyed up as he was by being in the middle of the enemy camp, he wanted desperately to lie down and sleep for about a week.

Instead, he tied the horse's reins to the hitching post in front of the house and climbed wearily to the porch. Under the serape, his right hand closed around the butt of the gun while he raised his left to knock on the door.

"Who's there?" The rumbling question came from inside, in Lobo's voice.

"Rios," Fargo said hoarsely, trying to sound as much like the segundo as he could. He added, "Capitán," to make it sound more realistic.

"Come in."

Fargo followed Lobo's command and stepped into the room, letting the door swing softly shut behind him. As he saw what was happening inside the house, he thought that there was no end to the surprises Lobo was capable of. Lobo and Juliana appeared to have just sat down to dinner at a table covered with a dazzlingly white linen cloth. The table was set with fine china and crystal glasses that sparkled in the light of the chandelier. Though small, the setting would not have been out of place in a fine home somewhere. In Mexico City, say.

Juliana looked lovely in a low-cut gown. Fargo didn't know where Lobo had gotten it. Stolen it from the baggage in some stagecoach robbery, more than likely. Lobo himself wore a black suit with a frilly white shirt under the jacket. He had a silk tie around his thick neck, and his hair and beard were combed. He was trying to make an impression, it looked like.

But judging by the tense expression on Juliana's face, it wasn't working. Not completely, anyway.

Lobo set aside a linen napkin and came to his feet, turning toward Fargo. "Did you attend to that little chore I asked you to do, Hector?"

Fargo knew what he meant and why he phrased the question that way. Lobo didn't want to come right out and ask if Rios had found Fargo's body, not right in front of Juliana this way. Keeping his head down, Fargo nodded without saying anything.

Lobo picked up the napkin, patted his lips, and murmured to Juliana, "I'll be right back, m'love. Just a bit of business to attend to with Señor Rios here." He came toward Fargo, his movements similar to those of a stalking panther.

Fargo didn't want Lobo to get too close to him, certainly not within reach of those long, powerful arms. But he had succeeded in drawing the man away from the table where Juliana still sat. It was time for the masquerade to end.

Fargo lifted his head, raised his left arm, and swept the sombrero with its silly dangling balls off his head. At the same time, his right hand came up with the gun and his thumb eared back the hammer as he leveled the barrel at Lobo.

"Don't move and don't yell," he said, "because if you raise the alarm, I won't have one good reason not to blow your damned brains out, Lobo."

10

The outlaw leader stiffened, his eyes widening in surprise as he stared at Fargo. Behind him at the table, Juliana gave a soft little cry and stood up. Fargo wanted to look at her and assure her that everything would be all right, but he didn't dare take his eyes off of Lobo.

Finally, after a long moment, Lobo seemed to relax. A smile even tugged at his wide mouth. "So," he said, "I take it you didn't make the acquaintance of El Gordo."

"If you mean that giant javelina, I killed him," Fargo said.

Lobo tilted his head to one side. "Really? I'm impressed, Fargo. One man, naked, armed only with a knife, and you killed not only El Gordo but also Hector Rios, as tough a man as I've ever known. Bravo, sir, bravo. You must be an utter savage at heart."

"No," Fargo said, "just a man who doesn't believe in giving up until the job is done."

"And what job is that?" Lobo asked, still smiling.

"You're going to get me and Señora Barrientos out of here alive. You'll be riding with us, and if your men come after us, I'll kill you."

"I think not," Lobo said, boldly confident. "Allow me to use your own logic against you, Fargo. If you kill me, my men will have no reason to hold back. They'll slaughter you without hesitation. Since you need me alive, your threats of death hold no force."

Fargo looked at him for a moment and then said, "All that may be true, but you're forgetting one thing, Lobo . . . you've put me through so much hell I might not mind dying if it meant I got to kill you first."

Lobo's confidence faltered slightly. Fargo saw it in his eyes. Trying to deal with a madman was always disconcerting and, at this moment, Lobo couldn't be certain that his adversary was completely sane. That was exactly the impression Fargo wanted to create in the brigand's mind.

"Come now," Lobo said. "I admire a bold man, a brave man. You could have ridden away from here and never looked behind you, and yet you risked everything to come back out of some stubborn, heroic ideal. Like a knight of old, you came to save the queen." He waved a big hand in Juliana's direction without turning to look at her. His voice hardened as he went on, "But you can't. She's going to stay here with me forever. The only thing you can do, Fargo, is save yourself, and I'm offering you that chance. Out of respect for your courage, I'll allow you to ride away. All I want is your word of honor that you'll never return to this place."

"You expect me to believe that you won't gun me down as soon as I turn my back on you?"

Lobo drew himself up haughtily and looked offended. "I make you a fair, nay, a generous offer, sir, and you throw insults back in my face? Here I am, willing to forgive the fact that you murdered a good friend and a loyal subordinate of mine, and still you goad me?" Lobo shook his head. "The offer is withdrawn. Go ahead and shoot me if you want to. Either way, you'll never leave this camp alive."

"John . . ."

Something in Juliana's voice finally made Lobo turn to her again. "What is it, m'love?"

Juliana was on her feet, with one hand resting on the table to steady herself. "John, please let me leave," she said. "Let Señor Fargo take me away from here. If you ever truly loved me—"

"If?" Lobo interrupted. "If I loved you? My God, woman, I've never loved anyone else *but* you!"

"Then let me go," Juliana whispered. "Otherwise, you don't really love me. You just want to possess me."

Lobo looked stricken. "You can't mean that," he said as he lifted a hand and held it out toward her. "All these years I've dreamed of being together with you again. I cannot let you go now. You'd be taking my heart and soul with you."

"I have begun to see that you have no heart. You have no soul."

Lobo's face flushed darkly with emotion. "Don't say that. You can't mean that."

"I do mean it," Juliana said calmly.

Lobo started to take a step toward her. Fargo said, "Don't move, Lobo. I'll shoot—"

But it wasn't Fargo who pressed the trigger. Somewhere outside, a rattle of gunfire suddenly erupted, the shots tumbling out, one on top of the other. Involuntarily, Fargo's tight-strung nerves jerked him slightly toward the door.

With a roar, Lobo wheeled around and lunged at him, swinging a long, massive arm. It slammed the gun in Fargo's hand aside just as he pulled the trigger. The bullet flew wide of Lobo as he barreled into Fargo.

Fargo had no idea what was going on outside, and he didn't have time to worry about it. He had more pressing problems at the moment, such as how to keep Lobo from getting those apelike arms around him and squeezing him to death. The gun had flown out of Fargo's hand when Lobo hit it, so now he was unarmed again except for the Arkansas toothpick. Before he could reach the knife, Lobo bore him over backward.

In an attempt to keep the bigger man from crashing down on top of him, Fargo twisted desperately in midair. He landed on his side on one of the thick rugs. Lobo was beside him, reaching for him. Fargo kicked Lobo in the knee and rolled away. Lobo let out a roar of pain and anger, and Fargo realized that, for the second time, he was fighting a massive beast full of killing hate. Unlike the giant javelina, though, Lobo had a cunning human brain. That made him even more dangerous.

Fargo surged to his feet and pulled the Arkansas toothpick from behind his belt as he tossed the serape aside so that it wouldn't hinder him. Outside, guns continued to roar. A full-scale battle was going on, from the sound of it, but in here the combat was more intimate, just Fargo and Lobo, with Juliana Barrientos looking on with an expression of helpless horror on her face.

Lobo climbed upright, grimacing as he put weight on the knee that Fargo had kicked. It held, though, and Lobo grinned. "You don't think that little knife's going to stop me, do you, Fargo?"

"Sounds like you've got more trouble to deal with than just me," Fargo replied, jerking his head toward the door. "Your hideout is under attack."

"My men will deal with that. Right now there are things to settle between you and me."

With that, Lobo began stalking forward, hands outstretched, fingers flexing in anticipation of grabbing hold of Fargo.

"John, no!" Juliana cried. "Please stop!"

Lobo ignored her. He rushed Fargo again. Fargo slashed with the toothpick, but Lobo wheeled to one side. The blade left a shallow gash on his left arm, but his right came around in a crushing blow to Fargo's head that sent the Trailsman sprawling against the chair where he had been tied up the previous night. That gave Lobo the opportunity to spring past him to the fireplace, where he reached up and ripped one of the old cutlasses down from the wall display.

"Now, lad, you'll see how a buccaneer fights!" he proclaimed triumphantly as he turned toward Fargo and brandished the cutlass.

Although the Arkansas toothpick was as sturdy as a sword, Lobo now had the advantage in reach. He came at Fargo, slashing back and forth with the cutlass. Fargo had his hands full parrying the blows with the heavy knife. He had to duck aside desperately from the ones he couldn't block and once was forced to leap into the air and draw his legs up to avoid a swift cut at his knees.

Alarm bells clamored in the back of Fargo's brain. He couldn't keep this up for much longer. He was too tired and his body was too battered. His reserves of strength were depleted. Any second now, one of his countermoves was going to be too slow, and the blade in Lobo's hand was going to hack into him, probably fatally. Lobo was so big and strong and fast that, if he got the chance, he was capable of lopping off an opponent's arm—or even his head.

Fargo gave ground until the backs of his legs hit the table where Lobo and Juliana had been about to dine. As Lobo's cutlass came flashing down in a stroke that would have cleaved Fargo's skull wide open, Fargo threw himself backward, rolling over the table. The cutlass hit the table and bit deep into the wood, sticking there for a second or two. As Lobo growled a curse and yanked it free, Fargo darted past him to the fireplace and reached up to grab the other cutlass. He swung around to face Lobo again.

"Think that'll help you, do you?" Lobo asked with that savage grin of his. "Ever used a cutlass before, Fargo? I've fought hundreds of battles with one."

"I'll take my chances," Fargo panted.

"Then I'll enjoy carving you into little pieces that much more."

With that, Lobo went on the attack again, his blade flashing in the light.

Although Fargo hadn't said as much, he *had* used a sword a few times in the past. He wasn't a complete novice with the weapon. But neither was he an expert—a far cry from it, in fact. He did the best he could, parrying Lobo's strokes and thrusting and slashing with his own blade when he got the chance. Lobo turned all those attacks aside with ease, though.

The cutlasses clanged together so loudly that the noise almost drowned out the gunfire. Sparks flew from the blades. Shards of light reflected from them as they spun and danced. Fargo's pulse hammered in his head. The muscles of his arm were leaden, but somehow he compelled them to keep working, to follow his mental commands as he struggled to hold off

Lobo's attack. Fargo circled warily, wondering if he could somehow get to the door and get outside, where he would have more room.

But that would mean leaving Juliana behind. She seemed rooted to the spot where she stood near the table. Fargo backed toward her, turning sideways to make himself a smaller target for Lobo's blade.

Suddenly, with a peal like that of a bell, steel rang against steel yet again, and Fargo felt the grip of the cutlass torn from his hand. It clattered onto the table. Lobo's superior skill with the weapon had finally won out. The outlaw leader slashed at Fargo's head on the backswing.

Fargo had no choice but to duck. He launched himself at Lobo's legs. It was about like tackling a couple of tree trunks, but Fargo was a big, powerful man himself. Lobo staggered back. He changed his grip on the cutlass and drove the blade at Fargo's back.

Fargo twisted aside but couldn't completely avoid the thrust. The blade sliced along his side and left a hot, wet line of agony. He slashed at the back of Lobo's left leg with the toothpick. The heavy blade cut deep. Lobo bellowed in pain as blood spurted and the leg folded up underneath him.

The man's massive weight landed on top of Fargo. Fargo heaved and rolled him off. Lobo reached out and caught hold of Fargo's right wrist, twisting until the knife slipped out of Fargo's fingers. Lobo let go and hacked at him with the cutlass, but Fargo rolled out of reach of the blade.

Now he was completely unarmed. Lobo was crippled, though. The brigand struggled to rise as Fargo climbed back to his feet. Lobo's left leg wouldn't work. Fargo had succeeded in hamstringing him.

Lobo didn't give up easily, though. He caught hold of the table with his free hand and used the cutlass in his other hand to brace himself as he slowly heaved himself back to his feet. He managed to smile as he said, "You fought a good fight, Fargo. This leg of mine may have to come off. But I'll replace it with a peg, and I'll be as good as new. Just you wait and see." He chuckled through his pain. "No, that's right, you won't be able to wait and see. Because you'll be dead."

"How are you going to kill me?" Fargo asked wearily. "You can't even move."

Lobo took his hand off the table. "I would have preferred to finish you off with good honest steel, but since I need this cutlass to lean on . . ." He reached inside his coat and brought out a pistol.

"You had that all along?"

"Of course. But, like I said, a pirate likes the keen edge of a sword."

Lobo raised the gun and pulled back the hammer.

Fargo tensed his muscles, ready to try to leap aside, out of the path of the bullet. It was a long chance, but the only one he had.

Suddenly, Lobo's eyes widened, and he said with a gust of breath, "Ah!" The hand holding the pistol sagged toward the floor. He struggled to bring it up and point it at Fargo again, but he didn't seem to have the strength. His head turned, and as he gazed in horror over his shoulder, he croaked, "M'love . . . how . . . how could . . ."

That was all he got out before he pitched forward onto his face. Fargo saw Juliana standing behind where Lobo had been. Her face was drained of color, and she had raised her hands to press them to her mouth. In front of her, the hilt of the cutlass that had slid down the table after Lobo's blade ripped it from Fargo's hand swayed back and forth. Several inches of the blade were buried in Lobo's back.

"He . . . he was a madman," Juliana said hollowly. "No matter what he said, no matter how he claimed to love me, he was insane."

Fargo nodded. "That's right, señora. He would have kept you a prisoner here for the rest of your life. You've saved your life, as well as mine. Gracias."

Fargo found the gun Lobo had knocked out of his hand earlier. He picked it up and holstered it, and then took Juliana's arm. "Go back in the bedroom and stay there," he told her.

"What are you going to do, Señor Fargo?"

He looked grimly at the front door. Beyond it, the fighting continued. "Whoever's out there, I reckon I'd better give them a hand."

Juliana jerked her head in a nod. As she started toward the bedroom, Fargo went to the door and eased it open. He saw muzzle flashes lighting up the darkness outside and went out the door swiftly, darting to the end of the porch and dropping off it to land in a crouch. The gun was in his hand again.

Shots came from the spot where the trail through the chaparral opened into the clearing. They were directed at the shacks where the members of the gang had taken cover. Return fire came from a couple of the shacks. The others were silent and appeared to have been riddled with bullets. Any defenders inside them were dead or seriously wounded by now.

Fargo began shooting toward the shacks where the last of the defenders were holed up. This attack from a different angle was the last straw for the embattled outlaws. They burst from their concealment, guns blazing, evidently determined to go out in a blaze of glory.

There was nothing glorious about the volley of lead that ripped through them. It was a quick, ugly death that sent the outlaws sprawling lifelessly to the ground.

Fargo stood up and began reloading the revolver with shells from the loops on Hector Rios' gun belt. The shooting had died away as the last of the outlaws fell, but Fargo called, "Hold your fire!" anyway, not wanting the attackers to mistake him for one of the gang.

Not surprisingly, Antonia Barrientos y Escobar burst from the trail and ran toward him, carrying a rifle. "Skye!" she cried. "Skye, is that you?"

"It's me," Fargo told her as several more figures emerged from the chaparral and came into the glow of the dying fire. He saw Elena and Ramona Barrientos, Rooster Jones, and big Jack Hagen and Alex Wilson from Dinero, along with several other citizens from that settlement farther south on the Nueces.

Antonia threw her arms around Fargo. He winced and grunted as his sore muscles and ripped-up hide protested, but Antonia didn't notice and Fargo didn't tell her to take it easy. It felt too good just being alive and holding her again.

Elena and Ramona came up to Fargo as well, while Rooster and the other men spread out to check on the outlaws to make sure they were all dead or at least out of the fight.

"It's mighty good to see you señoritas," Fargo told the young women. "How's your father?"

"Father Pascual at the mission in Dinero is caring for him, along with Señora Hagen and Señora Wilson," Antonia said. "The padre says that Papa will be all right."

Fargo nodded, very glad to hear that news. He liked Eduardo Barrientos, and it certainly wasn't Eduardo's fault that Johnny Lobo had been obsessed with his wife.

"Elena, are you all right? I reckon you must've met up with Rooster last night and the two of you got away from here."

"*Sí*, he was waiting for me when I reached the trail through the chaparral," Elena said. "We made it to the horses and got away before Lobo's men could catch us."

Rooster walked up in time to hear what she said. He added, "Then we lit a shuck for Dinero, figurin' we'd bring back a posse to clean out these no-good bandits. Didn't make it all the way there, though, 'cause we run into Antonia and Ramona and those other hombres already headed up here with the same idea in mind. We was hopin' we'd meet up with you, either here or on the trail."

"You got here at the right time," Fargo said. "And you did a good job of cleaning out this hornet's nest."

"Skye," Antonia said, "where is my mother?"

Fargo inclined his head toward the door. "In the house. She's fine, just shaken and upset. Lobo's in there, too." He didn't add that Juliana had killed the bandit leader, but the finality in his tone of voice indicated that Lobo was dead.

Only he wasn't, because at that moment, the door of the house swung open and Lobo lurched out. Juliana was in front of him, and he had his right arm wrapped tightly around her neck. The cutlass was still in his left hand, and he used it as a crutch as he stumped out onto the porch, dragging his crippled left leg.

Juliana's daughters all cried out in shock at the sight, and Rooster bit back a curse and lifted his rifle. Antonia, Elena, and Ramona were only a second behind him as they recovered from the surprise of seeing their mother in Lobo's grip. Their rifles rose.

"Avast there!" Lobo shouted. "Lower those guns, or I'll snap this pretty wench's neck!"

"Take it easy," Fargo said in a low, urgent voice to Rooster and the girls. He saw the other cutlass still sticking out of Lobo's back. Blood dripped from that wound to form a small puddle on the porch planks. Obviously the wound hadn't been enough to kill him right away after all, but if he kept bleeding like that, the injury might prove fatal yet.

The question was, would that happen before Lobo could kill Juliana? And could Fargo afford to wait and see?

"You've sunk my ship and killed my crew," Lobo said, "but I'll see you all strung up by your thumbs from the yardarm, you bloody Spaniards! You can't get rid of Johnny Lobo!"

Lobo had lost his mind completely, Fargo thought. He believed he was back at sea again, instead of in the middle of the South Texas brush country. But that didn't make him any less dangerous. If only Lobo would weaken enough from loss of blood so that Juliana could slip out of his grasp. Then Fargo and the others could open fire. . . .

Suddenly, Lobo's head lifted. "Hear that?" he said. "The sound of breakers on the shore! The sea is calling to me! The sea is callin' me home!"

His arm dropped away from Juliana's throat. She pulled out of his grip and ran sobbing into the arms of her daughters. Fargo palmed out the revolver on his hip as the barrel of Rooster's rifle came up again.

But Fargo didn't fire, and something made him say quietly to Rooster, "Wait."

"Wait?" the old-timer repeated in amazement. "What in blazes for?"

"He's no threat anymore."

Indeed, Lobo didn't even seem to be paying any attention to the others now. He stumbled to the edge of the porch and down the steps, almost falling several times before he reached the ground. Then he began to hobble toward the resaca, digging the point of the cutlass into the ground with each step to help support himself, then wrenching it free and continuing on his laborious trek toward the water.

"The sea, the sea," he said in a thin voice. "Home to the sea . . ."

"But that ain't the sea," Rooster said to Fargo. "It ain't even salt water!"

"It is to him," Fargo said.

The men from Dinero came up to join Fargo, Rooster, and the Barrientos women. They all stood quietly, watching as Lobo struggled to reach the lake. Finally, the massive brigand stood at the edge of the water. He lifted both arms and brandished the cutlass over his head, swaying on his bad leg. He gave an incoherent cry as he fell forward and the water rose in a great splash.

Only, to Fargo, it looked more like Lobo jumped, rather than fell. . . .

Jack Hagen started forward. "We'd better get him out of there before he drowns!"

Fargo stopped Hagen with a hand on his arm. As he holstered the gun, he asked, "Why?"

Hagen didn't have an answer for that. He stood there like the others, numb with horror, as a great thrashing stirred up the surface of the lake for long moments.

Then, slowly, gradually, the water grew calm again.

"That resaca's plumb deep," Rooster said into the silence. "We won't never find his body."

"I don't plan to look for it," Fargo said as he sat down on the steps leading to the porch. He leaned his head against the post that supported the railing around the edge and closed his eyes as a wave of weariness washed over him.

A moment later a warm hand slipped into his, and no sooner had that happened than someone took hold of his other hand. He opened his eyes, looked to his right, and saw Elena Barrientos. He looked to his left, where Antonia smiled back at him.

No matter how beaten up he was, he figured he had a mighty good reason—two of them, in fact—to get his strength back in a hurry.

LOOKING FORWARD!
**The following is the opening
section of the next novel in the exciting
Trailsman series from Signet:**

**THE TRAILSMAN #298
DEAD MAN'S BOUNTY**

*Colorado, 1860—one corpse, two fillies from
Heart's Desire, and a whole heap of trouble.*

The tall, dark rider reined his horse to a sudden halt.
Hand flicking to the Colt .44 on his right hip, he
squinted his lake blue eyes at the rocky butte rising
in the south—sunbaked and stippled with sage and
dwarf pinions.

Fargo had heard something.

The Ovaro pinto beneath him had heard it, too. The
horse held its head high, ears pricked, eyes wary.

Another faint crack, like a twig snapping, sounded
on the other side of the scarp. Muffled by distance, it
was still louder than the previous gunshot. Whoever
the shooter was, he was heading toward Fargo.

The Trailsman, as he was known throughout the frontier, swung his right leg over the saddle horn, kicked his left boot from its stirrup, and slid straight down to the ground. Dropping the pinto's reins, he quickly shucked his Henry repeater from its saddle boot and grabbed a spyglass from his saddlebags. Hanging the glass around his neck by a leather thong, he jacked a .44 round into the Henry's chamber, then jogged around behind the horse and began climbing the scarp.

The big, broad-shouldered man, clad in buckskins, undershot boots, and a broad-brimmed hat, with a red bandanna knotted around his neck, moved with a mountain lion's quiet grace.

Gaining the crest's bank in no time, he doffed his hat and lay between two boulders. Keeping his head low, he stared southward through the spyglass, using a spindly sage clump to shield the lens from the sun.

A mile south, a little-used freight trail ran along a tree-lined wash. Along the trail, what looked like a small buckboard wagon was barreling along behind a stocky horse or a mule. From this distance, even through the spyglass, the animal and wagon were little more than a brown blur behind which a sand-colored dust cloud rose.

Smoke puffed over the wagon. A half second later, a rifle crack reached the Trailsman's ears.

Tightening the spyglass's focus, Fargo saw that one of the two people in the wagon was firing a rifle at something behind them. Sliding the glass westward, Fargo saw a half dozen horseback riders crest a low hill and gallop down the other side, making a beeline for the wagon.

The riders whooped and hollered, firing pistols and rifles at the fleeing buckboard.

Fargo cursed and shortened the spyglass to include a broader field of vision. The trail would take the wagon around the east side of the scarp. If Fargo hurried, he might be able to cut off the pursuers and find out what the hoorawing was all about—if it was about anything and not just a passel of bored hardcases hornswoggling a couple of hapless farmers.

Fargo was down the scarp in half the time it had taken him to climb it.

He slipped the Henry back in its boot, the glass back in the saddlebags, and swung into the saddle. Putting his spurs to the pinto, he galloped straight along his previous course, the scarp falling away to his right, the trail appearing ahead. He swung the Ovaro onto the trail and stopped, peering south as his own dust caught up to him.

He could see little but the trail disappearing over the brow of a low rise.

A scream rose. A mule brayed.

Pistols cracked over men's jubilant whoops.

The thunder clap of a wagon tipping pricked the hair along the back of the Trailsman's neck.

Skye Fargo spurred the Ovaro into a gallop. Horse and rider bolted over the low rise. Spying the overturned wagon in a sage-carpeted flat ahead and left of the wagon trail, Fargo reined the Ovaro toward the wreck, giving the horse its head.

The wagon lay on its side, near a line of pines curving along the base of low buttes and a creek. Contents from the box lay strewn for twenty yards across the flat. The wagon's two raised wheels were still spinning. The mule lay on its side, tangled in its traces, blood glistening at the back of its head.

Fargo poked his index finger through the Henry's

trigger guard when female screams rose amidst the men's laughter. He saw one of the attackers drop his trousers and raise the skirts of one of the fallen women, a blonde, while three men chased the other woman toward the creek.

The second woman, a brunette, was topless. One of her pursuers whipped a cream-colored blouse over his head as he chased her.

"No! Damn you!" the woman near the wagon protested before a sharp, backhanded slap knocked her flat against the side of the buckboard. "Get your filthy hands off me!"

Hearing the Ovaro's thundering hooves, two men rummaging through the spilled contents of the wagon spun toward Fargo, alarm flashing across their bearded, sun-seared faces. As they reached for the pistols jutting from their hips, Fargo snapped the Henry to his shoulder.

The Trailsman had fired from the pinto's hurricane deck enough times that he timed the shots precisely to the stallion's fluid gate.

Both men danced backward, screaming, dropping their pistols, and hitting the ground in unison.

Smoking Henry in hand, Fargo leaped from the saddle while the Ovaro continued running on past the dead mule and the wagon. The Trailsman stopped, dropped to a knee, and aimed the rifle toward the man with the blonde.

The man turned toward Fargo, his pants down around his ankles, his member jutting up between his drooping shirttails. Hatless, he held a pistol down near his right thigh, staring toward Fargo with an angry, befuddled expression on his mustachioed face.

"What in Christ?" the man barked. "Who the hell're you?"

"Drop the shootin' iron," Fargo called from one knee, his rifle butt snugged to his cheek.

"Like hell!"

The man raised the pistol and stepped forward. Before he could level the .45, he tripped over his pants and his longhandles, and stumbled forward, triggering the .45 into the ground halfway between him and Fargo. The Trailsman triggered his own shot as the man fell, the bullet cutting the air over and right of the hardcase's head.

Lying on his right hip, raging, the man raised the revolver. As he thumbed the hammer back, Fargo's Henry spoke. The slug plunked through the center of the hardcase's forehead, an inch above his bushy, black brows, exiting his skull with a spray of brains, bone, and blood. The man fell back, staring sightlessly at the sky as his legs kicked spasmodically.

Fargo glanced at the blonde.

She sat with her bare feet and legs spread, skirt still bunched around her waist. She wasn't wearing pantaloons, only a skimpy pair of lacy pink underpants which the hardcase had torn in half, revealing the creamy curve of her left hip rising to a narrow waist.

In too much shock to bother covering her long, shapely legs, she glanced from Fargo to the dead hardcase then back again, her sandy brows bunched with befuddlement. Weed flecks clung to her long, curly hair. Blood trickled from a crack in her upper lip.

A pistol spoke. A slug kicked up dirt a yard from Fargo's left boot.

"Oh!" the blonde cried.

Fargo turned toward the shot. The two men who'd been chasing the brunette were now running toward the Trailsman, their pistols held high, long dusters flapping around their legs. The hat of the man on the right blew off as, running, he leveled the revolver, squinted down the barrel, and fired.

The slug sizzled past Fargo's left ear.

As the other man fired, Fargo levered a fresh shell into his Henry's breech. He snapped off an errant shot then, intending to remove the blonde from the line of fire, traced a serpentine course toward the overturned wagon, keeping the old buckboard between him and the two approaching hardcases.

As he ducked down behind the wagon's undercarriage, a bullet clanked and sparked off the iron-rimmed rear wheel. Another drilled through the box, missing Fargo by a hair's breadth. Tightening his jaws, he snaked the Henry over the wagon, aimed at the man approaching on his left, and drilled a ragged hole through the man's left shoulder.

The man screamed a curse and dropped to his knees, grabbing his bloody shoulder with the hand holding the six-shooter. Fargo ejected the spent shell, loaded another, and swung the rifle toward the other hardcase.

As the man shouted, *"Son of a bitch!"* and triggered a round through the slack of the Trailsman's left shirt sleeve, Fargo pulled the trigger, watched the bullet plunk through the man's lower chest. The bullet exited his lower back and spanged off a rock, painting it bloodred.

He screamed and clutched his back, triggering his pistol into the ground. The report hadn't yet faded when the Trailsman rammed another shell into the Henry's breech and swung back to the other shooter.

The man glared up at the Trailsman, jaws slack, sweat runneling the grime on his gray-bristled face.

"Wh-who the hell are you an'—an' why the fuck can't you mind your own *business*?"

"Name's Fargo." The Trailsman punched a slug through the man's right temple, slamming him back into the dirt.

Fargo turned to the other man, aimed the Henry. The man stared back at him, face bunched with pain and exasperation, small eyes open wide. Fargo raked, "Didn't your momma ever teach you how to act around girls?"

"No, wait!" the man cried.

Fargo sent a slug careening through his left cheekbone and watched the man's quivering head follow half his brain pan onto the gravel and sage behind him.

He looked around.

All the hardcases were down and unmoving, their horses and Fargo's pinto grazing back in the pines lining the creek. Fargo lowered his Winchester and tramped over to where the blonde lay in the sage where he'd last seen her. She looked around dumbly, let her gaze stray up to the tall, dark stranger. Fargo returned the appraisal, his heart giving a little hitch at all that thick blonde hair curling down her shoulders, at the cobalt blue eyes and small, round breasts pushing at the dusty orange blouse ripped halfway down her lightly freckled chest.

When his eyes trailed down from her wasp waist to her bare, creamy legs and small, fine-boned feet looking so pink and delicate amidst the gravel and sage, she gave a haughty chuff and jerked her skirt down over her knees and feet. Her eyes snapped wide, the befuddled veil lifting, and she turned to where the other girl lay at the edge of the pines. "Charity!"

The blonde pushed herself up and, holding her skirt above her bare feet with one hand, wove around shrubs and large rocks as she ran toward the creek. Fargo glanced at the torn, pink underpants she'd left on a tuft of silverthorn. His cheek twitched wryly, and he turned to follow her.

The girl's feet must be as hard soled as Modoc moccasins. She didn't falter once in spite of the tough, brown, prickly weeds and gravel.

She knelt beside the other girl called Charity, took the girl's hand in her own, and called her name. Fargo stopped behind the blonde. The brunette lay on her back. Her thick, auburn hair had partially fallen from the prim bun atop her head, and hung in dusty ringlets about her finely-sculpted, full-lipped face. The girl's blouse and corset lay in the weeds a good distance away. Her deep, full round breasts, pale as new-fallen snow and tipped with red-brown nipples, cast oval shadows down her belly.

The blonde sobbed and, clutching Charity's hand in both of hers, lowered her head over the unconscious girl's chest. "Charity! Oh, God, Charity—*please don't die!*"

She must have seen Fargo's shadow angling across Charity's legs. She whipped her head around and looked up at him, her blue eyes tear filled, brows furled with exasperation. "Would you please quit staring at her breasts, and *do* something!"